Catching A Pixie

Alleigh Burrows

CATCHING A PIXIE

Published in the United States of America
By Artemis Publishing LLC
P.O. Box 633
Springfield, TN 37172

Copyright 2020 by Alleigh Burrows
ISBN: 978-1-7354197-3-2

All rights reserved. No part of this work is transferrable, either in whole or in part. It may not be reproduced, stored in a retrieval system, or transmitted in any form or by any means, electronic, mechanical photocopying, recording, or otherwise, without the express prior written permission of both the copyright owner and this publisher. Scanning, uploading, and distribution of this book via any means whatsoever is illegal and punishable by law.

This is a work of fiction. Except for historical and famous characters, all characters, names, places, and events appearing in this work are a product of the author's imagination or used fictitiously. Any resemblance to real persons, living or dead, is entirely coincidental.

Dedication

This book is dedicated to my husband and children who believed that I'd get another book published, even when I did not. And thank you to the Valley Forge Romance Writers for their support, Karen for critiquing my master's student description, Beth for her unrelenting book promotion, and the kindly NY State Trooper who inspired this story.

Chapter 1

I was having a perfectly marvelous day until I looked in my rearview mirror and saw the flashing red and blue lights of a police car zooming up behind me.

On my way to Lake George to meet my friends for a weekend getaway, I had been happily cruising up the New York Thruway in my little Ford Fiesta. There were only a few cars here and there and I darted around them, eager to get to the cottage before dark. I didn't have a care in the world.

It was a beautiful afternoon in early September. The temperature was warm but not too hot. The trees, illuminated by the sun, glowed a fiery mix of crimson and gold, vivid against an azure blue sky. My favorite song has been playing and I was singing away like I was auditioning for American Idol. I felt like the queen of the road.

Until I saw the lights flashing in my rearview mirror.

Crap. Was that for me? Glancing down, I was amazed to see the speedometer just above eighty.

Double crap. I never speed.

Okay, that wasn't true. I do occasionally speed, but not because I like to go fast and show off how badass I am, or I think I'm so important that rules don't apply to me. I carefully go five, sometimes ten miles over the speed limit when I'm feeling particularly daring, but quickly lose my nerve and duck back into the right lane.

Not today. Queen of the road was about to get her crown handed to her.

I located a spot by the side of the road with a wide shoulder and pulled over. Despite my desperate hope the cop car would fly past me chasing some true evildoer, it pulled up behind me.

My pulse kicked up to about a hundred. I'd seen people pulled over on TV, so I sort of knew what to expect, but since it had never happened to me before, I was shaking. I gave a quick check of my front seat. Seatbelt on. Phone in my bag. No underwear sticking out of my luggage. I turned down my music and took a deep breath. *Okay, I can do this.*

The trooper got out of his car and slowly approached my passenger side. I pressed the window button, panicked when the rear window opened, and fumbled around to press the front button. He had stopped back near the door jamb, so I couldn't see his face, but I hoped he smiled at that—obviously no hardened criminal here. Finally, he leaned forward and peered into my car.

"Ma'am, do you realize you were speeding?"

My brain shut down. "Was I?"

"Yes, ma'am. Eighty-one in a sixty-five."

What was I supposed to say? *Sorry? Shit, really? Is there anything I can do to make this go away...and run my hand up my leg to show off some thigh?*

None of those seemed viable options, so I just shrugged and flashed him a hesitant smile. His straight-brimmed hat obscured his face, which made me even more nervous. I'd hoped to get a sense of how much trouble I was in.

"This your car?"

I nodded. When he didn't say anything, I realized he was waiting for me to speak. *Gah!*

"Um, yes, sir. This is my car."

"Can I see your registration?"

"Of course," I leaned over and pawed through my glove compartment until I found a crumpled up official-looking paper. "Is this it?"

He stared at me like I was a bit simple.

"Sorry," I pressed my hand over my racing heart. "I've been driving for eight years and never been pulled over before."

"So, no other violations?"

"God, no. Never. Not even a parking ticket." I leaned toward the passenger window, my voice cracking with distress. "I'm really sorry about this. I don't even know how it happened. I was following the flow of traffic and when the other cars turned off, I guess…I wasn't…I didn't pay attention. It was an accident. I swear I don't make a habit of speeding."

"Mm-hmm. License, please?"

Apologizing had no effect whatsoever. Bummer. Because it truly had been an accident. How could I have been this stupid?

I dug through my bag, pulling out my wallet. Still anxious, I had trouble getting my license out of the plastic covering.

As I handed it to the officer, I was finally able to see his face. Hmm, younger than I had expected, dark eyes, firm mouth, but with a hint of a smile. That was reassuring.

Then he glanced down at the license and his hat obscured his face again. "Your name is Lindsay Andrews and you live in Roselle, Delaware?"

"Yes," I said with a smile. He was looking at the license, after all.

He must have heard something in my voice because he gave me a piercing look. "I just need to verify."

Ouch. Properly chastised, I nodded.

"I'm going back to my car to run a check. Stay here."

Until he'd issued that command, it had not occurred to me to leave. Was it even an option? He had my license, after all. Did people drive off? Wasn't it obvious they'd get caught since he had their address?

He disappeared into his car and I sat there fidgeting in my seat as I waited for him. I checked my rearview mirror a few dozen times, tapping my fingers on the steering wheel, waiting. I chipped at my nail polish, waited, tapped some more.

After the twenty-seventh time I checked the mirror, I actually *looked* at my reflection. Yikes! What had happened to my hair? It was a mess, like usual. I really should get it cut, since it was always falling into my food or getting caught in the straps of my backpack. I just hadn't worked up the nerve to chop it off. I ran my hand through it, trying to smooth out the snarls before pulling it into a raggedy ponytail.

A second glance in the mirror didn't show much improvement. Jesus, was I really that pale? I was tempted to brush on some mascara but figured if he caught me, I'd look pretty frivolous. So, I went back to waiting, tapping, and chipping my nails.

He was taking forever and I started to get paranoid. What exactly was he learning about me? Did he know I got in trouble for petting a police dog during a mock emergency drill? Because, seriously, that had been my only brush with the law.

Finally, his car door opened. He strolled back to my window and leaned in. Handing me my license, he gave me an intense once-over.

"I should write you a speeding ticket," he said, "but your record's clean." He paused, rapped a pen on his notepad twice, and continued, "Your Delaware tag is partially obstructed by your Red Sox license plate frame. This is a violation in New York, so I'm going to write you a ticket for that, instead."

"Having a Red Sox plate is a violation? What, are you a Yankees fan?"

Ugh, don't be a babbling idiot!

He gave me that look again like I was simple. "Uhhh. No. It's a minor traffic violation, like a warning, so you won't be assessed points on your license."

I dropped my face into my hands and groaned with embarrassment. Peeking out from between my fingers, I mumbled, "Sorry, I'm epically nervous."

This time the smile reached his eyes. "Yes, ma'am. I can see that. Don't be. You just check the box on this form and pay a small penalty. No points. You'll be fine."

Taking a breath, I managed to regain my senses. "Thank you. That sounds much better…and cheaper."

And out of nowhere, he announced, "I went to Roselle University." He flashed me a sweet smile and I realized he was cute. Really cute.

Which made me all nervous and goofy again, so I blurted out, "Hey, I live in Roselle." Then giggled like a moron, because of course, he knew that. He'd seen my license. That's why he'd said it.

Trying to pull myself together, I said, "Oh yeah? Cool. When did you graduate?"

When he didn't answer right away, I thought maybe I'd gotten too personal. But he'd brought it up, right?

Finally, he responded, "Six years ago."

"Really? I got my undergrad there four years ago. Now I'm back, getting my master's in nutrition."

"That's great. Good for you." A charged silence settled between us and I waited, eager and still, for him to say something more. He looked like he wanted to. But instead, he tipped his finger to his hat in salute and stepped away from the window.

I guessed we were done. Too bad, because I felt like there was a strange spark between us. Which was silly, because he'd just pulled me over for breaking the law, but still…

Before I had a chance to raise my window, he leaned in again. "Drive carefully, ma'am. If you set your cruise control under eighty, you should avoid any future problems." Cute little crinkles formed around his warm, brown eyes and a dimple appeared in his right cheek.

Yowza. His dimple held a major heat factor and made me go all melty inside. I wanted to say something sexy or flirty but was unable to do more than mouth the words, "Thank you."

He seemed to have felt it too, frozen in place for a few heartbeats. Then he cleared his throat, tipped his hat a final time, and strode back to his car. I watched him go in the rearview mirror, his uniform accenting a very firm asset.

    He climbed in his cruiser and waited for me to edge out into traffic. Then, with the lights still flashing, he followed me onto the Thruway. I glanced over when he passed by and I could have sworn he gave me a little wave.

Chapter 2

Roselle University's homecoming game was in early October, yet when I got up Saturday morning, there was frost on the window. I had to dig out my coat and mittens before loading up the cooler and heading to my best friend Gabby's place.

I knocked on the door and let myself in. Gabby was buzzing around the kitchen trying to do seven things at once. Always excitable, she threw her arms around me as soon as I walked through the doorway, almost knocking me down. I couldn't help laughing. She was a tiny little thing, but always a constant blur of brown curls and enthusiasm.

I barely got in a hello before she launched into her mile-a-minute conversation. "Hey, Lindsay, where have you been? I just got a text from Ashley. She and Kirsten are at the stadium already. She's saving us a parking spot near the field house. She said it's pretty chilly out, and we should wear layers."

She returned to the kitchen table and grabbed an oversized knife, gesturing toward a mound of vegetables on the cutting board.

I slid the ragged carrots onto the veggie tray and handed her a head of broccoli to annihilate. "Yeah, I noticed. I wore a coat, but now that I cut my hair, my neck got cold." I'd worked up the nerve to cut it über short. I thought it looked much more mature than my long, black ponytail, but it was taking some getting used to.

"I'll grab you a scarf. You can start slicing the mushrooms." She handed me the knife and darted over to the closet. "It should warm up by noon, but no point in suffering if you don't have to."

She threw the scarf at me and turned to stuff the vegetables, subs, and assorted snacks into a blue cooler. "I like your hair, by the way. The change is a bit shocking, but it really suits you. Makes your eyes look—I don't know—dramatic."

Gabby had always been jealous of my long, totally straight hair, so, I was pleasantly surprised she approved. She hated her curly brown hair, which she called frizzy, but I considered bouncy, just like her. I was going to say thanks, but she had already headed into the dining room.

"One more thing and I'll be ready," she sang out and reappeared with a bottle of Jägermeister.

"This will keep us warm." She smiled and tucked it into the bag.

Girlfriend thinks of everything.

We loaded the food into my car and headed for the stadium. Ashley, always the master of efficiency, had saved us a spot next to her SUV. She'd already set up chairs, covered the table with homecoming decorations, and started the grill. Kirsten was stretched out on an inflatable chair, enjoying a beer and staying out of her way.

"Hey, bitches!" Ashley hollered as we got out of the car. She wrapped me in a hug and then did a doubletake. "Oh, Linds, I love your hair!"

"Thanks." I tugged at the strands at my neck, self-consciously. "You don't think it's too short?"

"Oh, no. It suits you. Makes you look like a little pixie."

"Uhh, thanks." I knew she meant it as a compliment, but still. I'd hoped to portray a capable professional, not a fairyland creature.

Kirsten was more subdued in her greeting. "Hey, chickie. How you doing?" She waved a hand in my direction while remaining in her chair. The contrasting personalities between the two best friends was remarkable—especially since they looked so alike, they could have been sisters. Tall, blond, and athletic, they'd intimidated me to no end when I'd met them sophomore year. But after a get-to-know-you social in the residence hall, we went out and got hammered, and the rest was history. Best friends for life.

We finished pulling everything out of the car and huddled our chairs together, stamping our feet and sipping Jäger, trying to maintain feeling in our fingers and toes. Ashley, in her usual fashion, waited until I had tipped a glass to my lips before blurting out, "So, Linds, how's your sex life?"

Shouda seen that one coming. But instead, I half-swallowed, half-spit the mouthful of Jager. Barking out a cough, I wiped my face and grimaced. "Nonexistent, as usual. Thanks for asking."

She grinned, a wicked glint in her eye. "C'mon, girl! You gotta get out there, Find a man…or a couple of them."

I snorted. "Seriously, Ash. I'm shy and awkward and have no game. You know that. Unlike you, I don't have men falling all over themselves to be with me."

"True. It's a curse I have to bear." She tossed her hair over her shoulder with a smirk. Then like a lioness going in for the kill, she verbally pounced. "If you would get out a little, socialize, I'm sure you could find someone."

"Fat chance," I sighed. "Between school and work, I barely have time to sleep, let alone date."

Ashley leaned her chair back on two legs, waving her hand airily. "Then don't work so hard. Cut back on your work hours and just finish your classes.

As if it were that easy. "I can't do that. I've got bills to pay ya' know. Not all of us have a rich daddy to support us."

She snorted, not the least bit offended. "Whatever. I'm sure your mom makes enough to support you for a few months. You *know* she must be giving Sean money."

I groaned. "I do not want to be like my brother."

She choked out a laugh. "I didn't mean it like that. You could never be like Sean. He's a slug of major proportion."

"Hey! He's not so bad," Gabby protested. When we stared at her, she flushed. "He's just a late bloomer, that's all. He'll find his way, eventually."

Gabby was a second-grade teacher and couldn't help pointing out the best in people.

But Ashley was right. Sean was a year younger than me and one of the most unmotivated people I'd ever known.

"Linds, all I'm saying is you should scale back a little. Have some fun. Enjoy your last few months of school."

"But I enjoy working hard. And my work is allowing me to create the perfect job at NutraHealth. They are helping to fund my master's degree so I can oversee their new pediatric program when I graduate. It's an amazing honor and I want to do it right. Besides, I'm twenty-four—too old to sponge off my parents."

"I *like* sponging off my parents," Kirsten announced with a grin. Her unexpected proclamation broke the tension and we laughed. She had a great job and only lived at home because she traveled all the time.

I patted her cheek and she winked at me.

"Look I'd love to have a social life. But even if I did find someone fabulous, the odds of being able to catch his eye, *and* hold his interest while studying for my master's are depressingly minuscule. Which means, for now, it's nose to the grindstone time."

"Too bad you didn't get that state trooper's number. He sounded like a hottie." Kirsten grinned.

I bobbed my head in agreement. "He was pretty impressive."

I'd told them about the cute cop who'd pulled me over. Rolling my glass between my hands, I thought back, picturing the way he looked. The way he acted. And got that melty feeling again. "I don't think he meant to flirt with me, but he did. I could tell it embarrassed him. Which was sweet." With a grin, I added, "And boy, did he fill out a pair of pants."

"Lindsay!" Gabby gasped. "That is definitely not like you."

"Well, I usually don't notice, but the way he sauntered back to his car, with his holster slung low on his hips…mmm. If I'd thought I'd meet him again, I might have considered speeding all the way home." I raised my glass in the air. They hooted and clinked my glass.

Kirsten leaned down to pick up the bottle of Jager and gave me a refill. "Well, I hope you can find someone as fabulous in Delaware. You deserve it."

"Thanks, hon."

I had to admit I was a bit jealous of the well-balanced lives they'd established after graduation. Gabby had the perfect teaching job and was now dating a "nice Jewish boy" that her mother strongly approved of. Ashley worked in New York City and spent her free time and sizable paycheck enjoying a whirlwind of activities. Kirsten's job required her to travel a lot, but she still managed to have fun. Meanwhile, I rotated through a never-ending cycle of going to class, the library, work, and home to study.

But today was different. I was tailgating with my besties and determined to enjoy the time.

Tired of everyone dissecting my personal life, Gabby grabbed the sub tray and passed it around while Kirsten heated up her famous gumbo on the grill. Ashley set up a table of red cups for us—and channeling our college days—displayed some mad beer pong skills. Attracted by the noise, a few other Roselle grads came over to join in and things started to get pretty raucous. Ashley always attracted a crowd.

That's not really my thing, so I grabbed Gabby. "You want to wander around? I think Sean's got a tailgate around here somewhere."

She ran both hands through her hair, relief clearly evident on her face. "Sure. Let's go before things get out of hand."

I called out to Kirsten, "We'll be back in an hour or so." When she waved us goodbye, I grabbed two beers from the cooler, and Gabby and I set out across the field.

A few rows over, I spotted one of my brother's friends playing cornhole. "Hey Nick, where's Sean? He's coming today, right?"

He paused in mid toss; his mouth twisted like he'd swallowed a bug. "Yeah, he's parked over by the north end, hanging with his lacrosse buddies. I guess we're not good enough for him." He threw the beanbag and it sailed right over the wooden target.

I smirked, enjoying his irritation. "Well, you're not. Learn to deal with it. Maybe if you'd picked a cool sport instead of wrestling, he'd want to spend more time with you." Nick had been friends with Sean since third grade, so he was like another brother to me. It was always fun to yank his chain.

"Yeah, yeah." He swirled his hand around as though holding a fairy wand. "Like skipping around a field waving a stick at people is cool." His next throw banged the bottom edge of the cornhole board, making his teammate groan. He flipped him the finger.

I giggled. "Well, it's better than wearing onesies and rolling around with other dudes."

When he turned his finger in my direction, I couldn't resist getting in one final dig. "C'mon Gabs, this tailgate is lame. Let's find us some hot lacrosse players." We linked arms and headed for the other side of the stadium, laughing as Nick recommended we engage in an inappropriate sex act.

The north end was packed with cars, but I managed to spot Sean gathered around a grill with his former teammates. Typical guys, they were all in T-shirts and jeans, not a sweatshirt in the bunch. Meanwhile, I was still bundled up in a coat and mittens—thankfully, since the cold beer I was holding would have turned my fingers numb.

We waved at him before settling into a pair of vacant folding chairs they'd set up across the way. We had just started a heated debate over which local bar served the best guacamole when Gabby grabbed my arm. "That guy is checking you out."

I whipped around. "Where?"

Keeping her hand near her lap, she pointed across the way. "Down there. See Sean by the grill? There's a tall guy to his left, sitting on the bed of a green pickup truck."

I glanced over. Hmm, cute. Well built, nice smile, not bad. But also, not looking at me.

"No, he's not."

She shrugged. "Well, he was."

A minute later, she nudged me again. "Linds, he is definitely checking you out."

I rolled my eyes. "Get real. My face is red and chapped from the cold. My hair's sticking up everywhere—" I yanked off my fuzzy red mittens and ran my hand through to smooth it back into place. "No one could find this attractive."

She gave me the once-over only a close friend could give and declared, "You look amazing."

Grateful for the support, it gave me the confidence to peek over again and this time he was looking. Our eyes met and he flashed me a smile before turning his attention back to his friend.

I giggled like a five-year-old. "Ooow. He was! Now, what should I do?"

"Why don't you grab a fresh beer, run on over there and tell him he should get to know you better?"

I gawked at her. "You know *that's* not going to happen."

Gabby patted my arm. "I know. You're totally pathetic and will simply sit here, wasting a perfect opportunity and he will never learn how fabulous you are. But whatever—your choice."

Ouch. The truth hurt. I sat there thinking maybe I *should* make a move when, the next thing I knew, Sean was walking over with a couple of his buddies. And he had that guy with him.

Chapter 3

"Hey, Linds. How are you?" Sean called out.

I got up and gave him a hug. "Good, how about you?"

"Not bad. A little cold."

Duh. He was wearing a t-shirt. The only one with any sense was his cute friend, who seemed all warm and toasty in a cream-colored cable knit sweater, jeans, and work boots. Yum.

Sean motioned to the guys next to him. "You know Charlie and Mike, right? And this here's Matt. He's down from New York." Then he waved an arm in my direction. "This is my sister Lindsay and her friend Gabby."

Matt was a tall one, over six feet. I had to tip my head up to look at his face. His warm brown eyes locked with mine, and a smile crept over his face. It was then I noticed the hint of a dimple in his cheek. And it hit me.

Unable to keep the grin from my face, I held out my hand. "Hello, officer."

His smile grew wider. "Hello, ma'am."

He shook my hand, and a tingle shot up my arm. His grip was firm and confident and when I glanced at his hands, they were so…manly. I have a thing for hands. And these? Well, these were hands I could fantasize about.

I returned my gaze to his face and my heart did a funny little loop-de-loop. He had a strong jaw, some seriously sexy cheekbones, and a smile that made my knees go weak. His hair was short, but not too short, and brown with kind of golden highlights. I'd thought his eyes were brown too, but they appeared amber in the sunlight. And they were focused on me—as though I were the only person in the world.

He dipped his head. "I thought I recognized you, but couldn't be sure. Your hair is different…shorter."

I couldn't believe he'd noticed. I reached up and ran my hand through what was left of it. "I got it cut last week."

Sean's head swiveled between us before turning to his friends. When they shrugged, he turned back to me. "Do you two know each other?"

I tried to be casual about it. "Well, sort of. This is the guy who pulled me over last month on the Thruway."

"No way!" Gabby waggled her eyebrows as she nudged me with her elbow. "This is *The Guy*?"

I rolled my eyes at her. "Yes. This is the guy."

Matt grinned at our exchange. "So, I'm 'The Guy'? What does that mean?"

I nudged Gabby back, trying to shut her up. "Nothing. It means nothing. Gabby, this is Matt, the *officer* who pulled me over, and nothing else."

Sean stared at us as though we were talking in a foreign tongue. Subtlety was never his strong suit. He shrugged and said, "Great, he's the guy. Whatever. We're going to take a leak. Feel free to hang out until we get back. There's beer and shots in the cooler and dogs on the grill. Help yourselves."

With a wave, he headed over toward the port-a-potties.

"Hang on. I'll go with you," Gabby called out. She flashed me a smirk and took off running. Her mother would be proud of that little *yenta* maneuver. About as subtle as a sledgehammer.

I stood there alone with officer hottie; my heart started beating like a snare drum. I desperately fought to form a coherent thought but came up empty.

He did not appear to suffer from the same affliction. "Would you like a hot dog? They're getting a little crispy over there and I'd hate to see them go to waste." Matt motioned across the way.

"Sure." I trailed after him like an adoring puppy. How could I not? He walked as though he could conquer the world, all ramrod straight and in control. And boy, could he fill out a pair of jeans. He was simply gorgeous, front and back.

When he got to the table, he motioned for me to sit on the tailgate of his truck. As I did, he dug out two rolls, pulled hot dogs off the grill, and turned to me. "Do you want ketchup or mustard?"

He was waiting on me. How sweet! Then I realized he wanted an answer. "Uhh, ketchup, please."

He squeezed two careful squiggles on the dogs and handed me one. We sat there, quietly, taking surreptitious measure of each other as we ate until I couldn't take it any longer.

"So, how have you been?" Weak, I know, but that was all I could think of. Fortunately, he played along.

"Good. How are you? No more speeding tickets?"

I laughed and bumped his shoulder. "No."

His expression turned serious. "I wasn't sure if I should acknowledge I knew you today. I didn't want to embarrass you if you hadn't told your family about being pulled over.

I laughed. "Oh, no, I told everyone how nice you were not giving me a speeding ticket."

He made a face. "Ugh, that's supposed to be a secret. You can't let people know police officers have a heart."

"Sorry." I grinned. "You know, I'd never been so panicked in all my life."

"I could tell. You were so cute; I couldn't bring myself to hit you with a big fine."

"You thought I was cute?" My heart rate tripled to hear him say it.

He gave me an exasperated look. "Yes. And since I'm *That Guy* to your friends, I can assume you found me not-hideous as well."

"Definitely not hideous. Certainly tolerable."

His mouth twitched. "Tolerable, huh? I'll try not to let that go to my head."

I giggled, struggling to come up with a witty response when Sean returned.

Gabby, seeing me sitting next to Matt, flashed me an excited grin and turned her attention to Sean. I wasn't sure if I wanted to thank her or smack her for not coming over to offer support.

Just as the guys pulled fresh beers out of the cooler, a burly security guard walked up wearing an ugly brown uniform and a scowl. "The football game is starting. Time to go in," he announced.

Sean sat down and raised a beer at him in salute. "Sorry, sir. We don't have any tickets."

The guard wasn't going to be put off that easily. He folded his arms across his chest and said, "New rules. Didn't you hear? There's no tailgating during the game. You need to go inside or pack up."

This stirred up a chorus of protests. "But it's homecoming."

He didn't alter his belligerent expression. He'd probably heard it a million times today.

Charlie howled, "You've got to be kidding me. We're all graduates, and not disturbing anyone."

Apparently, that wasn't the issue. With an arrogant smirk, the guard repeated, "That's not my problem. No tickets, no tailgate. Everyone has to leave."

Charlie—always the hothead of the group—took this as a personal affront. He stepped forward.

The guard squared up.

The air became charged.

Oh God, this was going to get ugly. Fast.

In a flash, Matt placed himself between the two men. His stance was so authoritative, both men froze. Adopting a tone with the perfect combination of respect and assertiveness, he said, "Please excuse my friends. We were only hoping to enjoy ourselves for a little longer. If that is not possible—" he paused to let the guard respond.

While he'd relaxed his aggressive posture, the guard did not offer a compromise. Matt held his gaze, and I could sense he was trying to will the man to change his mind. When that didn't happen, he said tightly, "Don't worry officer. It's fine. We'll leave."

He turned back to us, his expression impassive. "C'mon. We can go to the Raven."

"But!" started Charlie.

Matt cut him off with a wave of his hand. "The man's just doing his job. We have to go." His tone brooked no argument, and with only minor grumbling, the guys started to pack up their gear.

Wow. Impressive. When Sean's buddies get worked up, there was usually a fight.

But Matt managed to defuse the situation in seconds. He was truly swoon worthy. And I decided I wasn't about to let him get away that easily. I'd have to invite myself along.

Right on cue, my phone buzzed. I pulled it from my pocket. It was a text from Ashley

We just got shut down. We're heading to Main St. How about you?

I showed it to Gabby and she nodded.

I typed in: *Us too. Going to the Raven.*

Ok. C ya.

The Raven was a dive of a bar where the college kids go. One side was dominated by a dark, dinged-up mahogany bar with mismatched stools and a ginormous mirror running along the length of the wall. The remainder of the room was crowded with wooden tables and booths, creatively decorated with years of graffiti carved into their surface. If you're hoping to reconnect with old friends, that's where you'd go.

I called over to Sean, "It looks like our tailgate was rousted as well. How about we join you at the Raven, okay?"

He dumped the cooler into the bed of the truck. "Sure. Whatever. See you over there."

I flashed a hesitant smile at Matt and he gave me a wink. *Squeee.*

Gabby linked arms with me and whispered. "Girl, you were right. He is hot! And he likes you."

"I think so, too."

Chapter 4

By the time Gabby and I weaved our way back to my car, most of the other tailgaters had packed up. We maneuvered out of the parking lot and followed the line of cars to Main Street.

As expected, the Raven was packed with a jovial crowd all vying for space at the bar. As soon as we walked in, Gabby spotted Ash and Kir and darted over, disappearing into a tangle of limbs.

I'm slower to get acclimated and stood in the doorway to get my bearings while streams of people filed past me. It only took a moment before I felt a very tall presence behind me. Tilting my head to the side, I spied a cream-colored sweater inches from my right shoulder. *Hot damn. He came.*

"Wow. It's really crowded." Matt shouted in my ear.

I grimaced and waved my hand toward the mob. "There's not much room at the bar."

"No," his voice deep and somber. Then he touched my elbow and gestured toward the side near the kitchen. "I think I see some empty tables over there. You want to sit down?"

"Uh, sure." An excited tingle flitted down my spine. I couldn't believe he wanted to sit with me instead of hanging out with his friends.

Matt approached the hostess and she escorted us to a small table tucked behind a pole. On the way, I caught Gabby's eye in the midst of a boisterous group. I gave her a little finger wave and she flashed me a thumbs up.

Once we were seated, it took a few minutes for a haggard, young server to fight her way over.

"What can I get you, two," she hollered.

Matt turned to me, "What would you like?"

"I'll take a Coors Lite."

Twisting back toward the waitress, he repeated, "The lady would like a Coors Lite and I'll have a Coke, please."

"A Coke?' I repeated with surprise.

"Yeah. I've gotta work tomorrow, so I have to be on the road pretty early."

Which meant he was leaving. Tomorrow. Bummer. I don't know exactly what I had expected to happen—but another day or two would have been nice. Or five...

Unaware of the misery he'd dropped in my lap, he turned to the server and reiterated, "We would like a Coors Lite and a Coke, please. If it's not too much trouble."

"Sure thing." Her smile brightened at his polite request and then she scooted through the tables.

"Do you mind me drinking beer? I could switch to soda."

"No, it's fine. Just make sure you are careful driving home."

How cute, he'd sneak in a cop warning. I crossed my hand over my heart. "I promise. I won't drink more than one an hour, officer."

He cringed. "I didn't mean it like that."

I patted his arm, enjoying the solid feel of muscles under the wool. "I was only kidding. I like how you are so authoritative. It certainly helped smooth over that business with the security guard."

"Well, I've had some practice. That lacrosse group can get pretty intense."

Looking over toward the bar, we witnessed the guys tossing back shots and chest-thumping each other.

Matt shook his head, as I sighed. "So, how do you know my brother and his insufferable friends?"

He shrugged. "I don't know Sean well. But I roomed with Charlie's brother during college and the lacrosse guys would all hang out at our place, so I've bumped into him a few times."

"Wow. You mean it was only a wild coincidence we ran into each other today? Amazing."

He blinked. "Uhh, yeah."

"What?"

A sly grin caused his dimple to emerge. "Well, the truth is, the reason I came to homecoming was I was hoping to see you. I knew you were a student here, so I thought maybe…"

What? I couldn't keep the grin from my face. "You're kidding. There was no guarantee I would even *be* here."

"Yeah, I know." He looked embarrassed. "I guess I got lucky."

With a hesitant smile, I whispered, "Well, I'm glad you did."

"Me too."

Our eyes locked and I felt a tantalizing sizzle pass between us. Yowza! He had great eyes. Now that we were in the dimly lit bar, they were dark brown. It gave me a silly, happy feeling inside to know they'd turn amber again outside—like I knew a secret about him.

"I think you said you were getting your master's degree," he blurted out, breaking the awkward silence that had fallen. "What do you want to do with that?"

Tamping down my hormones, I tried to put my brain back in gear. "Good memory. I'm going for Health and Nutrition. With a master's, I'll be able to create nutritional interventions to help my clients modify their behaviors."

He stared at me with a blank expression.

Yeah, I get that a lot. "I teach people how to eat better, so they stay healthy."

"Ahhh. A very worthy cause." His dimple appeared again. I had to grip my hands together to stop from running my finger across his sexy divot. My self-control was weakening when the server popped up and placed our drinks on the table.

"Do you need anything else?" she directed her words at Matt, with a flash of teeth and a flick of her hair.

He didn't seem to notice. "No, we're good, thanks."

She paused a moment, willing him to focus on her, but when no further attention was forthcoming, she left with a pout. *Good.*

"Our waitress was making eyes at you."

He didn't break his gaze from me. He simply shrugged and took my hand. "I'm making eyes at you. Is that okay?"

Sigh. "It is way more than okay." Then my insecurities surfaced. "Can I ask why?"

His brows crinkled together. "*Why?* Like why am I interested in you?"

I nodded.

He rubbed my palm with the pad of his thumb, giving his answer careful consideration. Then his eyes locked with mine, a hint of nervousness lurking in their depths.

"I know we just met, but I like you. I think you're sweet. A little shy..." The corner of his mouth lifted in a silly grin. "You're only a little bitty thing, which I find adorable."

"Really?" I'm about five foot nothing and built like a twelve-year-old boy. Bitty, yes, but adorable?

"Yup." He wasn't done. "Your eyes are an absolutely mesmerizing color blue. They are unbelievably sexy."

Unable to resist, I fluttered my eyelashes.

"Nice. That makes it ten times worse."

I laughed. This was fun. "What else?"

He took a sip of his soda. Calmly. Enjoying the moment. Then put the glass down and continued. "Let's see. Sweet. Huge blue eyes. Lips kissable as hell." He paused to let those words sink in.

Once he mentioned them, my lips went dry. When I licked them, his eyes went dark. Darker. Almost black. My blood began pounding as he moved closer, his gaze stopped on my mouth.

Then he sat back and grinned. "Plus, I like your nose."

"What?"

He leaned forward and tapped it with his index finger. "Your nose. I like how it curls up at the tip, like a pixie."

Oh God, what was with me and pixie comparisons today?

"So, you like pixies?"

"Oh yeah. I *love* pixies. My mom has them all over the house. They've got big soulful eyes and very short skirts. They caught my interest as a sex-crazed youth and I've never gotten over them."

His wolf-like grin took my breath away. I managed to suck in enough air to ask, "So, looking like a pixie is a good thing?"

Reaching for my hand, he raised it to his lips and kissed my knuckles. "Mmm hmm. A very good thing."

I blushed. Right there in the middle of the Raven, I blushed like a teenager. This day was turning out to be too delicious.

He must have felt the same sizzle as I did because he withdrew his hand and plucked at his thick cable knit sweater.

"Wow, it's really warm in here." He wiped his hand over his forehead, then pushed up the sleeves of his sweater, giving me a glimpse of his forearms. Damn, even they were nice. I could see the veins bulging against the muscles in his arm. Now *I* was getting overheated. It had been a very long time since I'd been with anyone and I was having some definite blood-pumping urges right there in the middle of a crowded bar.

I took a big swig of beer to try and cool down. When that didn't work, I took another one.

As I put down my glass, a guy brushed past our table and then stopped with a shout, "Hey Quin, how ya doin'? Long time, no see."

Matt smiled and stood up. "Hey, Murph. I'm good. How are you?"

"Good." Murph seemed pretty solid, but as the two men shook hands I couldn't help noticing Matt had him by about four inches. I'd never been too impressed with height—considering everyone is tall to me—but seeing Matt tower over this guy made my heart go pitter pat all over again.

"Where are you stationed, DSP?" Matt asked.

"Yup, troop six in Elsmere. You still in New York?"

Matt nodded, "State trooper for the Thruway. I'm hoping to transfer into investigative work eventually, but this will do for now."

They chatted for a moment before Murph stole a quick glance at me. "Well, Quin, it looks as though I might be interrupting your evening. How about if we talk later?" Flashing Matt an insolent grin, he slapped him on the back and drifted away.

Matt returned to his chair, "That was Murph. We served an internship together at the Delaware State Police during college. Good guy."

I smiled and took a sip of beer. "Yes, he seems it. Why'd he call you Quin?"

Matt coughed and got a strange expression on his face. "Well, that's kind of a funny story…"

My stomach did a nervous flip. "Funny, *ha ha* or funny *weird*?"

His gaze slid somewhere around my left ear. "Weird, probably." Huffing out a breath, he said,

"Here's the thing. My last name is Quinsy." A grin appeared. "Matt Quinsy."

He let the words sink in. As they began to process through my slightly beer-soaked brain, I looked up at him in horror. "You mean?"

He nodded and his smile grew wider. "Yup."

I started again, "So if we…"

He nodded. "Yup."

I gulped. "If we wound up together, I'd be Lindsay Quinsy?"

He laughed. "That would be correct." Then he paused, before adding, "Lindsay Quinsy. I kinda like it."

I groaned and dropped my head in my hands. Without warning, the giggles started. A few punctuated bursts at first, but as soon as I thought I'd gotten them under control, I'd look up at his ridiculous grin, and they'd bubble up again. Soon, he started to laugh too. Feeding off each other, there was no way we could stop.

"Oh, my sides hurt," I moaned between outbursts.

He wiped tears from his eyes. "It isn't that funny, ya' know."

"Yeah, I know."

"It's not like…" He was going to say, 'it's not like we were dating or anything.' And suddenly, a little of the magic went out of the evening.

"Yeah," I echoed, "It's not…like it matters, I guess."

His eyes dropped to his glass and he began to trace circles in the condensation, distracting me. *God*, he had sexy hands—strong, with a light dusting of hair, long fingers, neat nails. I could imagine those fingers tracing circles over my naked body.

Hoo, boy. I was way too excited thinking about that. And just my luck, I'd never get the chance to experience it. Because he was leaving. Tomorrow. And I'd probably never see him again.

As for tonight? Well, I wasn't that kind of girl. Dammit.

Maybe I could be? *Just this once?*

No, I sighed. Definitely not. I wished I could be, but I'm not.

Chapter 5

Depressed thinking about how little time we had together, I suddenly felt exhausted. Trying to be discrete, I turned to watch my friends still hanging at the bar and yawned so wide my jaw popped.

"Boring you, am I?"

So much for being discreet. Luckily, Matt had a smile on his face. Still, it was a little embarrassing. "God no. I'm having a great time. But, being outside all day, drinking…it wears me out.

It didn't seem to bother anyone else. Gabby, Kir, and Ash were having a blast bouncing around the bar. Sean's buddies were shouting insults at each other, having an awesome time. And I was with the most intriguing man I've ever talked to…and yawning in his face.

Which meant he was going to leave at any moment and I'd never see him again.

Right? Or would I?

"Do you get down to Delaware very often?" I asked, embarrassed by the pathetically eager tone in my voice.

He grimaced and leaned back heavily in his chair. "No. Most of my college friends were from out-of-state, so I only come back for the occasional alumni event."

With a hopeful look, he asked, "Do you drive up to New York very often?"

I shook my head. "Once or twice a year to visit my friend Ashley's cottage in Lake George. That's where I was headed last month." We sat there, deflated, letting the hum of voices circle around us.

Suddenly, the volume rose and a flood of people began heading for the door.

Gabby stumbled by me, looking pretty looped. I was her ride. I couldn't imagine where she thought she was going.

I started to get up when Kirsten darted past and grabbed her arm. Before I could move, Ashley came up behind me and laid a hand on my shoulder.

"Don't worry, Linds. We'll get her home. You stay and have fun."

I started to argue when she pressed me down into the chair. Waving a warning finger in my face, she barked, "Don't move. We've got this." And she disappeared through the door.

"Who was that?" Matt craned his neck to watch the blond blur march off.

"No one."

I wasn't about to introduce her to Matt. Over the years, I'd hooked up with a few guys whom I'd really liked. Everything would be fine until they'd meet Ashley. She was damn impressive—tall, blond, charismatic—a force of nature. And my pathetic boyfriends would be drawn to her. She never did it on purpose, and she never acknowledged their interest, but afterward, I could tell they were only hanging out with me to be around her. There was no way in *hell* I was going to introduce her to Matt.

As she disappeared, a passel of drunk men suddenly descended upon us. Charlie stumbled into the table. Fumes of alcohol wafted over the table as he bellowed, "Matt! Hey, Matt, my man. You ready to go?"

Now it was Matt's turn to look startled. He steadied his glass before it tipped over and croaked, "Go? I thought you were having a good time here."

"Nah, dude, this place is dead." As if to emphasize his point, Charlie swung his arm around and almost took out three people. His friends snickered.

Struggling to remain calm, Matt dropped his head into his hand, pinching the bridge of his nose. "Are you sure? We could stay here a while longer."

"No, man. Let's bounce. Sean headed over to Kilarney's. Said it's rockin'. Everyone's there."

"Sean left?" I looked around. The jerk hadn't even said goodbye.

When I turned back to Matt, he shot me a glance full of regret. "I'm their designated driver." I knew his disappointment was echoed in my eyes. I *really* didn't want the evening to end.

Apparently, neither did he. "You want to join us?" He asked, his voice pitched low, barely audible over the din of the bar.

Tempting as it sounded, I knew I didn't have it in me. After a day of drinking, I was bone tired. I opened my mouth to answer and the words were overtaken by a yawn. I tried to smother it, then yawned again. "Sorry. Long day."

"I hear ya'. I'd rather not go either." His dimple was nowhere to be seen now. He stroked the back of my hand with his thumb as we shared a moment. Until Charlie banged on the table with his fist. "Matt! C'mon man. It's like TTG. Time to GO!"

Matt waved his hand, dismissively. "Yeah, yeah. Just give me a minute. Why don't you wait for me by my truck?"

With wavering eyes and a crooked smile, Charlie gave Matt an exaggerated wink. "You got it, buddy. Don't be too long. Don't want to freeze my nuts off out there, while you're busting yours."

Whoa, how embarrassing.

Matt narrowed his eyes and growled, "Charlie, one more word out of you, and I'm going to kick your ass. We clear?"

Charlie saluted Matt with a smirk, then turned and goose-stepped toward the door. As the rest of Sean's friends staggered away, Matt forced a smile at me, "Sorry. I should go."

I sighed. "Yeah, that's probably for the best. Good luck tonight."

"Thanks. I may need it," he said, rolling his eyes. "Are you ready to leave? I can walk you to your car."

"I would love it."

He threw some money down on the table and helped me to my feet. Then he grabbed my coat from the nearby hook and held it up so I could slide my arms in.

Sparkles of pleasure rippled over me as he followed me to the door. When was the last time someone held my coat for me?

Stepping outside, a blast of cold air buffeted us. After roasting in the steamy bar, it felt refreshing at first, but it didn't last long.

"Cold?" He laughed as I shivered. He wrapped his arm around me, leaned in, and whispered, "Good. I was hoping for an excuse to touch you."

It felt funny walking next to him. He was so much taller than me, I could rest my head against his chest. And his hand barely reached my waist. But he was warm, and he smelled nice, and I couldn't have been happier. Until we arrived at my car and reality set in.

"Lindsay, I..." He sounded so earnest; I couldn't help but smile.

"Yes?"

"I had a really good time tonight."

"Me too." I took a step closer and shifted my gaze up, up, up, from his chest to his jaw and then all the way up to stare into his eyes. We were standing in the yellowy glow of a streetlamp and it cast his face into soft shadows. Still, I could tell his eyes were locked onto mine and I shivered with anticipation. *Kiss me. I really, really want you to kiss me.*

A tentative smile crept up his face as he pulled me into his arms. He lowered his head, stopping a heartbeat away from my lips. Waiting. Questioning. It was torture.

I threw my arms around his neck and pulled him down. His sigh of relief caressed my cheeks an instant before his lips touched mine. Warm, soft, and delicious. He shifted his weight to draw me closer as he slid his tongue in my mouth.

My knees grew weak. They really did. I'd never had that happen before.

Then he pulled away…rested his forehead on mine…took a deep breath and huffed it out.

"Well, ummm, good night," he murmured.

I laughed, feeling as disappointed as he sounded. "So, you live in New York."

"Yeah." He rubbed his nose against mine. "Up near Albany."

"Is that where you pulled me over?" I ran my fingers through his hair, silky yet stubbly.

He nodded, murmuring into my cheek, "Not too far. About ten miles west." Then he kissed me again, soft lips warm on mine. More regretful than passionate. "And you live in Delaware. Four hours away."

A sad sigh hummed from my chest. "Kind of a long commute for a date."

"Any chance you were planning to move to New York in the next month or two?" He raised an eyebrow.

"That would make it tough to get to class every day."

"I guess." His shoulders slumped beneath my hands.

There was no future for us—just one magical day. My heart sank into a tight little box, pinched on all sides. "Well, it was nice meeting you, Matt Quinsy."

He gave me a crooked smile. "It was nice meeting you too, Lindsay not Quinsy."

I lowered my eyes and desperately searched for something to say. Something poignant or romantic or memorable. But nothing came to me. The best I could do was choke out, "Well, goodnight."

He wrapped me in a fierce hug, smelling of outdoors, wool, and man. I inhaled, determined to sear his delicious scent into my memory.

This was totally unfair.

He released me, opened my door and I climbed in. Unexpected tears pricked my eyes. "Bye," I whispered.

"Bye," he answered, before closing my door. He waved and turned away. I watched as he walked to his truck, shoulders hunched in the cold. His buddies swarmed around him, punching his arm and jostling him around before stumbling into their seats.

Too depressed to drive. I sat there, fighting back tears as he pulled out of the lot. It had been a perfect day, talking with a perfect guy, feeling a real connection, and now he was driving out of my life.

God damn it! I hadn't met anyone as amazing in forever. And he lived four hours away. Four hours! There was no way we could make that work with my schedule.

I wiped away a pathetic tear, took a deep breath, and drove home. Alone.

Chapter 6

"Hey, Linds, did that cop ever call you?" Sean yelled the question at me from behind the beer taps. Then he darted off to the other end of the bar before I could answer.

For some reason, Wednesday nights were always packed at the Raven. Ordinarily, I wouldn't be there on a school night—or at all, really—but dad had asked me to stop by on my way home and drop off some beef jerky he'd just made. He was freakishly proud of his jerky, so I was compelled to hand-deliver it ASAP.

I sipped my orange juice and waited for Sean to return. He had worked at the Raven in college and now picked up an occasional shift whenever he needed money. Or adoration. It was embarrassing to see the number of girls waving at him, flicking their hair, cooing their drink requests at him. And he flirted back, flashing his crooked smile, raking in the tips. And phone numbers. Ugh.

He scooped up a handful of bills, stuffed them in the register, and turned back to me. "Sorry. So, the cop?"

I knew I only had a few seconds, so I kept it brief. "Nah." I took a sip on my straw. "He was nice, but it wouldn't be practical."

"Practical? Jesus, you don't have to marry the guy. Just invite him down a few times, bone him, and cut him loose."

I gaped at him, mystified how we'd come from the same family. "Bone him? You are actually telling me to bone a complete stranger?" I waved my hand in front of his face. "Hellooo. This is your sister you're talking to."

He smirked. "That's right, I forgot. He'd be lucky to get to second base after a year of marriage." Without waiting for a response, he took two steps to his left and leaned over the bar to take another drink order. Holding two glasses under the beer tap, he waited for them to fill, while I stewed.

I wasn't that bad. Was I? I'd had boyfriends. We'd had sex. Not a lot, but enough. I was always more focused on work and grades. Meanwhile, Sean had skated through school on a lacrosse scholarship and charm.

"I'm back." He leaned his forearms onto the bar and squinted at me. "Seriously. Did you like him, Linds?"

I groaned, running my hand through my hair. Staring down into my glass, I nodded. "Yeah. I really liked him."

When a customer called Sean's name, he held up a finger and kept his attention riveted on me. "Linds, you don't always have to be practical. He seemed like a good guy. You should call him. See where it goes." And he trotted away to fill another order.

You should call him. Right. How would that go, exactly? Hey there, remember me? I know we agreed dating wasn't possible, but I thought I'd say hi and maybe…what? Have hot sweaty phone sex?

My head flopped into my crossed arms resting on the bar. Embarrassment made me weak. There was no way.

"Linds!"

I jerked up to find Sean standing in front of me, holding out his phone. "I texted Charlie. He gave me Matt's number."

My stomach gave a weird flip. Panic? Anger? I didn't know. But as he waved the phone at me, I couldn't resist snatching it from his hand.

Sean - *Do u have Matt's phone #, the NY trooper?*

Charlie – *Why, you in trouble?*

Sean - *No dude. Just helping my horny sister hook up.*

"*Sean*! You're such a pig." I screeched.

Unrepentant, he oinked, flashed the smile that had gotten him out of trouble with countless women, and strode down the bar to pour a row of shots.

I wanted to be mad. But glancing behind me to the table where Matt and I had sat, I knew he was right. Everyone was right. I deserved a little fun.

Before I could lose my nerve, I pulled out my phone and entered Matt's number. Sucking down the last of my juice, I laid a ten-dollar bill on the bar next to Sean's phone and climbed off the stool. I knew he wouldn't be happy accepting my money, so I blew him a kiss goodbye and quickly walked out of the bar.

When I got to my car, I pulled out my phone and climbed into the driver's seat. The streetlight glinted off my phone in my hand. *Our* streetlight. Where Matt and I had kissed.

A sign, perhaps?

I glanced at my dashboard clock, almost hoping it was too late to call. Nope. Only eight-thirty. Heat flushed my skin despite the cold temperature. No more excuses. I was going to do this.

Taking a deep inhale to calm my jitters, I pushed call. Irrationally, I checked my reflection in the rearview mirror while his phone rang. He couldn't see me, but knowing I looked okay gave me a jolt of confidence.

"This is Matt." His brusque tone shot through the phone.

Flustered, I stuttered out, "Uh, hey, this is Lindsay." Silence stretched out on the other end. "From Delaware."

He gave sort of a grunt before saying, "Yeah, hey. Hold on." More silence. Then I heard muffled male voices, footsteps and a door slam.

"Okay, I'm back. What's up?"

Not exactly the welcoming tone I'd been expecting. I floundered, not certain where to go from here. "Uh, nothing. I just…uhh…I had a good time the other day. And..uh…thought I'd call and say hi."

I heard rustling on the other end but then silence. Long enough for my brain to consider a whole list of self-flagellating names regarding my embarrassing stupidity.

"Oh, hey," he finally responded. "Sorry, I didn't expect to hear from you. How are you?"

He sounded moderately more interested, so I pressed forward. "Good. Busy, but that's nothing new. How about you?"

He didn't speak, but I could hear muffled yelling in the background.

I shifted uncomfortably in my seat. "I'm sorry. Did I catch you at a bad time?"

"No." A huff of breath crackled in my ear before he reversed his statement. "Well, yeah, actually."

Unsure how to respond, I waited for him to say more. The cool night air was seeping through my thin sweater and I shivered. "What's going on? Anything you want to talk about?"

With a dark, ominous chuckle he said, "No. Me and my dad are…let's just say we're having a difference of opinion." He mumbled something like *stubborn bastard* under his breath. He sounded pretty pissy, so I thought it best to move on.

"Well, I only called to say hi."

"Yeah, hi. It was nice hearing from you."

Then nothing. Bone-chilling silence. Embarrassed at how badly I'd obviously misread our relationship, I couldn't wait to get off the phone. Damn, Sean, for putting me up to this.

"Okay, then. Sorry to have interrupted. I'll let you go. Good luck with your father." I pushed the off button without waiting for a reply and threw my phone into my bag.

Once my hand was empty, I scrubbed my face in disgust. Stupid, stupid, stupid. Why couldn't I leave well enough alone? It was time to take my pathetic ass home. I turned on the ignition and my car lights illuminated the spot where Matt had kissed me. On the perfect night with the perfect man; I'd thought. *Blah!*

Chapter 7

Thank God it's Friday.

My shift at NutraHealth had ended and I couldn't wait to head over to Gabby's for movie night. We were going to watch *Zombieland* and pig out on chili. Kind of a gross pairing, but we were looking forward to it.

I pulled out my phone to ask her if I needed to bring anything, and 3 missed calls appeared on my screen.

Matt. The jerk. I certainly didn't need to hear from him. He'd already ruined one night—I'd spent six hours tossing and turning on Wednesday, replaying every second of our illusionary relationship and the painful brush off that followed.

He'd called twice Thursday, and apparently again today. There was no way I'd let him put a damper on tonight. I swiped away the notifications and called Gabby.

"Hi, girlfriend. I just got off work. You want me to pick up some wine or maybe a loaf of Italian bread?" I could hear the radio blaring in the background. I'd probably interrupted her dirty dancing around the kitchen as she prepped the meal.

"Nope. I'm good. Everything's ready. Get your *tuches* over here so we can start the movie."

That made me smile. I'd picked up a couple of Yiddish words from Gabby. *Tuches* was one of my favorites. "Yes, *bubalah*, I'll be there in about fifteen minutes."

I made good time and pulled into her parking lot with four minutes to spare when my cell rang. I grabbed it and pressed talk. "Sorry, chickie, but if you need something, it's too late. I'm right out front."

"Uhh, I'm not sure who 'chickie' is, but it's not me."

My pulse involuntarily jumped at the sound of Matt's voice. I tamped down my ridiculous hormones and forced out a cool response. "Oh, sorry, I thought it was my *friend* calling. Who is this?" Glancing in my mirror, I smoothed my hair in place, checked my teeth for food.

"Aww, come on, Lindsay. You know it's Matt. I've been trying to get a hold of you for two days. I wanted to apologize."

My heart sang, but fortunately, my brain quickly gained control. "For what? I came on too strong, calling you out of the blue. Obviously, I made you uncomfortable. It won't happen again. Now, if you'll excuse me, I have plans." I pulled the phone away to disconnect the call, but his urgent response stopped me.

"Wait!"

Aw, what the hell, my brain conceded. It couldn't hurt to listen. I returned the phone to my ear. "I'm still here."

He whooshed out a breath. "I wanted to say I'm sorry about how I reacted the other night. I was in the middle of a never-ending argument with my dad and my head was in a bad place."

"Hmph." Not good enough to merit a less grudging response. Noticing a layer of dust on the dashboard, I pulled a tissue from my purse and swiped it off. Waiting.

He cleared his throat. "See, my dad had a heart problem a few years ago. He's supposed to take it easy, but he won't listen to me when I tell him to relax. He tries to do stuff behind my back, and I find out, and I yell and he yells and it's a whole big thing." He stopped. Sighed. His sexy baritone voice dropped a tone. "But I didn't mean to take my temper out on you. I'm sorry. I was really glad you called."

He sounded sincere. I figured I could give him a little leeway. "All right. I forgive you, I guess. Just don't let it happen again."

"I promise. Scout's honor." I imagined him holding up three fingers and smiling. That sexy dimple on full display.

I suddenly pictured us sweaty and sated in my bed, where I would run my finger over his muscled chest, hoping to coax out that dimple. His eyes would darken and we would...

Goosebumps flashed over my skin. Damn, it looked like Sean was right. I'd only spent one day with the guy and I was ready to jump into bed with him. I had it bad. Squirming in my seat, I choked out the only thing echoing through my brain. "I'd like to see you again."

The silence was deafening. Shit, I'd done it again. I dropped my head onto the steering wheel. But he'd called me, right? What kind of game was he playing?

Finally, he cleared his throat. "I don't know what to say, Lindsay. I like you. I really do. And if you lived closer, I would definitely want to see you. But between work and my family and your school obligations..." Remorse bled through his voice. I wasn't imagining that. But he was right. Every minute I'm not studying, I'm at NutraHealth, helping to set up the new pediatric program. Driving four hours to see him and four hours back was out of the question. A totally impractical use of my time. *Damn.* This was so unfair!

"How about this?" His voice startled me out of my pity spiral. "There's no need to jump into a whole intense dating thing. Why don't we just talk when we can. See where it goes. You know—friends."

Friends. Not ideal, but not the worst thing either. My brain was happy with the compromise, but the rest of me was pretty disgruntled. I suppose it would be better than nothing. Not by much, but it would do. For now. So, I mustered up a cheerful falsetto and answered, "Sure, we could be friends. Keep it casual. See how it goes."

"Exactly." He sounded pleased by the prospect. "There's no need to jump into a whole thing. We'll just keep it light."

"Light. Yeah." I echoed, choking back my disappointment. I knew this was the right decision.

My phone buzzed against my ear. I held it out and a text from Gabby popped up.

Are you coming?

Apparently, no time soon, I sighed.

"Look, Matt, I've got to go. Gabby's waiting for me."

"Okay, sure, no problem." He paused before adding in a low husky voice, "Linds?"

"Yeah?"

"I'm really glad you called."

I melted, barely able to squeeze out a response. "Me too." *Ha!* Understatement of the year. "Bye."

I clicked off the phone and skipped up the stairs to Gabby's place.

Chapter 8

Five days later, I was sitting in my kitchen trying to force integrative holistic healthcare therapies into my brain when my phone buzzed.

I didn't recognize the number and almost let it go to voicemail. But frankly, I was eager for a distraction.

I pressed the Talk button.

"Hello, Lindsay? This is Matt. Matt Quinsy."

Oh my God. *Matt*. Play it cool and hope he can't tell I'm doing a happy dance in my chair. I'd picked up my phone a half dozen times this week to call him, but afraid I would appear too eager, I put it down each time. Score one for restraint. "Hey, Matt. How are you?"

"I'm fine. I uhh…I'd been thinking about you and just wanted to say hi."

He sounded a little unsure of himself, which—from a big, solid hunk like him—was adorable. I smiled. "Hi."

Matt cleared his throat. And then...nothing. Not a word. I waited. No way was I going to jump in and scare him away. I sat there, biting my tongue, my attention cartwheeling around the room. Hmm, what's that smudge on the cover of my textbook? Honey mustard maybe? Or au gratin sauce. Hard to tell. I grabbed a napkin to rub it off.

"It's my mom's pixies, you know." He blurted out.

What? My hand froze in mid-rub.

Quickly realizing how odd he'd sounded, he added, "That's why I had to call you. All those damn pixies staring at me in the kitchen." His voice deepened. "I could barely make it through a meal without thinking about you."

Delight bubbled in my chest like champagne. Awww. He'd been thinking of me. Really and truly. "That's sweet. I've been thinking about you, too."

"Good," he hummed into my ear. "So, umm, what now? What should we talk about?"

I laughed. "I don't know. You called me. What do you want to talk about?"

"I don't know. Politics?" I could hear the amusement in his voice, "Religion?"

The goofy grin on my face grew wider. "I don't think we're ready for that. How about something simple? What did you do today?"

"Fine." He let out an exaggerated sigh. "If that's the best we can do." I heard furniture creak as he switched positions on the other end. "I worked. Patrolled the Thruway, filed some paperwork, the usual."

"Wow." I twirled my pen in the air like a mock cheerleader. "Police work sounds thrilling."

He grunted. "Sometimes. Sometimes not."

"Tell me then, why did you go into law enforcement?"

Without missing a beat, he said, "Well, it's a good way to pick up women."

His response was so unexpected I snorted. I mean, he did pick me up, sort of, but I hardly thought he made a habit of it.

"Judging by your ladylike response, I assume you don't believe me."

"Sorry, I try not to snort until at least my third date." He had the sexiest voice. How had I not noticed that before? Too keyed up to sit still, I stood up and started pacing through my apartment. First into the living room, five steps later, the bedroom, then back into the living room. I sank into my favorite battered recliner and leaned back, amazed how relaxed I was talking to him. I'm usually all tongue-tied with men, but with Matt I felt...comfortable.

Comfortable enough to press him. "Are you going to answer my question? Why did you become a cop?"

I heard him shuffle around again. I pictured him, too, stretching out on an oversized chair as he considered how to respond.

"Truthfully, I want to help people. You know, serve, protect and defend. It's always a challenge dealing with people. But in a good way."

"Good answer. I guess I like nutrition for the same reason. I get to talk with people, coach them, help them."

"What will you do when you finish your master's?"

I pushed back in the chair until I was practically horizontal. I could literally sit like this all day and talk to him. "I'm a registered dietitian, and I've worked at NutraHealth for three years. Right now, I counsel adults with diabetes, helping them manage their nutritional needs." I smoothed down the corduroy on the chair's arms, turning the nap a consistent color.

Was I talking too much? Apparently not, since he didn't interrupt, so I added, "They said if I got my master's they'd put me in charge of the new children's unit they're adding to their Middlebury clinic. I love kids. It was too good an opportunity to pass up."

"Nice. Will you move down to Middlebury then?"

I gave a little fist pump. *Sweet*, he really had been listening.

"I don't know. I like Roselle. It's such a cute town and it's close to my family. I don't want to go too far." In Delaware, far is a relative term. Middlebury is only about thirty minutes away, but because it's "below the canal" it's considered a whole different region. Glancing over at my bookshelf littered with picture frames, I knew I'd have trouble moving anywhere else. There were photos of me playing pee wee soccer, mom and dad cheering at Sean's first lacrosse game, pictures of us stretched out around our pool or hugging each other on holidays. I loved every one of them.

"How about you? Do you have a swingin' bachelor pad in New York?"

He laughed. "Hardly. Actually, I live with my parents. I told you, my dad had a health scare a few years ago. I moved back home to help out—shoveling snow, cutting the grass, stuff like that."

Damn. Sexy, strong and caring? If he kept racking up the points in the perfect guy counter, I was going to have to make some serious life decisions.

"You're a big sweetie pie, offering to look out for them."

"Yeah, well, my brother and two sisters are all married and have families of their own. It just made sense for me."

"You are the youngest?"

"Yup, that's me. The baby."

I tried to picture such a big, imposing guy as a baby. "I have this sudden image of you crammed into a racing car bed, covered by a fluffy, white baby blanket, with Little League trophies staring down at you."

He barked out a laugh. "Nope. King-sized bed, navy blue and red comforter and not a trophy to be seen. I told you, the only thing staring down at me are my mom's pixies."

"I'd like to see them sometime." I'd blurted it out as a joke, but the strained sound from the other end of the phone let me know I'd once again crossed a line. Shit. I jumped up and started prowling my apartment again. *Friends…* I smacked my forehead. *He'd insisted we be friends.*

I wound up in the kitchen and collapsed in a chair next to my wall of textbooks. "Sorry, I…uh…didn't mean it like that, exactly." My heart was jammed up into my throat, making it difficult to talk. "I'm not some crazy stalker chick, who's gonna show up at your doorstep." I dropped my head into my hands, my face hot with embarrassment. "Seriously, I'm facing a bitch-load of classwork, working at Nutra-Health *and* developing my senior thesis. I don't have time to drive to New York."

"No, Linds. I should be the one to apologize. It's not you, I swear." Matt sighed as though the universe rested on his incredibly broad shoulders. I peeked out between the fingers cradling my face. Waiting.

"I guess I should come clean with you." He murmured, seemingly to himself. Then in a stronger voice, said, "The truth is, I was in a long-distance relationship once. After college."

The pause that followed pressed a weight—heavy and hard—against my chest. "And?" I squeaked out.

"And it didn't go well. Obviously. We went in different directions—literally and figuratively. It was really hard."

I could hear the bitterness behind the words and feel the painful sting as if it were my own.

Before I could say anything, he cleared his throat and his tone became softer. "That's why I'm hesitant to move this forward. The problem is, I like you, pixie girl."

Awww. My heart pitter-patted against my ribs. He had a nickname for me. Pixie girl. Ashley's ridiculous suggestion drifted back into my brain. *"Why don't you have some fun? Enjoy yourself."* Grrr. Like it was that easy. Nothing was easy for me. He didn't want a relationship. I didn't have time for a relationship. What was the point? None. This would never work. Except...

"I like you too, Matt."

There was no getting around it. Now the ball was in his court. Would he lob it back to me or pack up his racket and go home?

"Hey," he said, suddenly. "Maybe I could help you with your studying. Quiz you on nutrition stuff. Make sure you stay on top of things."

Seriously? He was offering to help me with my course work? Not at all practical, but it was cute that he offered. Hot damn, I was still in the game!

Giddy at the thought, I wiggled like a puppy in my chair. "Sure, why not. Look, I've got classes during the day and I work until about six o'clock. Then I hit the books the rest of the night. You don't have to quiz me, but a study break around eight would be much appreciated."

"Eight o'clock. Roger that."

I could hear the smile on his face. Picture his dimple. And a quiver shot through my long-neglected body part. Then I looked down and found my integrated therapies textbook glaring at me. "I should probably get back to studying."

He groaned, which made me feel a little better. "Yeah, I should do some laundry. Luckily, there are no pixies in the basement to torment me."

I smiled. "I'm really glad you called."

"Me too."

"Well, I'll talk to you tomorrow. Eight o'clock."

"I'll be here." After he hung up, I was tempted to sit there and doodle my sort of, almost boyfriend's name in my notebook, but integrated therapies weren't going to learn themselves. With a sigh, I picked up my highlighter and turned to chapter twelve.

Chapter 9

Hey, where are you? I texted to Matt on my way to class.

In between silly daydreaming about my non-boyfriend boyfriend, I had been managing to squeeze in studying between classes, but it wasn't easy. We'd quickly fallen into the habit of sharing silly texts and snapchats when we had a spare moment. In addition to the occasional phone calls, he'd been sending me ridiculous online nutrition quizzes with bogus answers which made me laugh.

A few seconds later my phone buzzed with his response.

Mile marker 70.

I giggled. He'd pulled me over there. I quickly responded. *What? On the thruway? Should you be texting on the job?*

I'm not driving ;)

Just lying in wait for unsuspecting coeds, so you can pull them over and date them?

Haha you caught me. But I've wised up and now only pull over women with NY license plates.

Hey!

J/k. You were my only traffic stalking.
Stalking?
Traffic stop stalking – get it?

I snorted so loudly, people walking past looked at me funny. Embarrassed, I buried my face into my coat and increased my pace. *Haha that was horrible*

I know. Shouldn't you be in class?
On my way. Get back to work. Stay safe, k?
Yes ma'am. Stay smart, k?
Yes sir. TTYS

This budding relationship had me all jittery and excited, like twinkle lights were flashing in my brain. I had to admit, I didn't hate it. In fact, things had been going so well, I was building up the nerve to suggest a visit. I had a rare free Saturday coming up. I floated the idea to Gabby when we met up after my morning classes.

"You should definitely ask him," said Gabby sipping her double expresso with mocha cream. "You can't tell me he's not interested. Look at all those texts! He's dying to *shtup* you."

"Shtup me?" I choked on my dark roast coffee. "How romantic."

She waved her hand, flicking her fingers twice in my direction. "Romance, blowmance, you need to get laid. Look at you. You're a mess!"

Stubbornly, I flopped my head backward to stare at the beveled tin ceiling of our favorite luncheonette, Roselle-a-deli. We'd come here for years, sitting at the pretty hand-painted tables and chairs, savoring the smell of home-baked bread, as we shared our joys and sorrows over freshly brewed coffee.

Today was both a joy and sorrow. I knew if I looked down, it wouldn't be pretty. I was wearing my brother's high school lacrosse shirt—once black, now faded to old concrete, navy blue sweatpants, pink socks with dancing hippopotamuses—fortunately, they both matched—and Ugg slippers. My laundry day had come and gone about three times this month. To be honest, I was lucky to be wearing underwear.

I moaned, running my hand through my hair. "I know, Gabs. But it's not as though I get days off every month like you. What's today? Columbus Day, Veteran's Day? I can't even keep track. I'm so jealous of your teachers' schedule."

"It's Columbus Day." She scrunched up her nose. "But teachers still work hard, you know. Sure, I have off today, but I'll be spending all weekend painting scenery for my students' fall concert." She picked up a spoon and idly stirred her nearly empty coffee. "Sean's going to help me."

A smile flickered across her face and I knew she didn't mind dedicating her weekend to her kids. She loved her job. Just like I would once I finished school and could have some time to myself. "But that's my point. You get random days off when you can meet me for lunch, run errands, take a nap. I feel like I have no free time, ever!"

"Well, I do have to have dinner at my mom's tonight, so my life isn't all chocolate and roses."

I laughed at her sour expression, giving her arm a sympathetic pat. Her mother was a handful. Nothing Gabby did was ever quite good enough. "Okay, you have me there. I'd much rather study the metabolic system than run the gauntlet at your mother's kitchen table."

"Amen, sistah." She clicked her mug against mine and downed her coffee. "Now, getting back to your man-problem…what's your plan? Are you gonna order him to get his cute little ass down here or just show up at his front door and drag him into his bedroom, while his parents listen from the living room?"

"Ewww." I buried my face in my hands. Then as I dragged my fingers through my hair, moaned, "I don't know. First, I have to find out if he's off on Saturday."

Gabby reached over and smoothed down the hair I must have pushed up into spiky horns. "If not, you could speed up the Thruway and hope he pulls you over again. Then get him to drag you to his police car for resisting arrest." She waggled her eyebrows at me. "That might be pretty hot."

I snorted. "I'm pretty sure I don't want to break a two-year dry spell by doin' it in a nasty old police car."

Gabby's eyes flew wide. "Two years! *Gott in Himmel*, girl, you should be grateful to get it anywhere."

When Gabby uses Yiddish, it usually makes me smile. Not this time. I took a bite of my sandwich, hoping to dull the hollow feeling pressing at my chest. It had been two years and seven months, but she didn't need to know that. It wasn't a big deal. In truth. sex had never been that fabulous when I was getting it.

But as I pictured Matt—all broad-shouldered and sexy—sauntering out of my shower, heading toward my bed, I got a funny, fluttery feeling inside. I had a feeling *fabulous* might be an understatement.

But not likely to happen any time soon. "The last time we discussed getting together he was adamantly against it. Said long-distance relationships didn't work, so there was no point."

"Yeah, but that was before all this—" she waved at my phone, showing bubble after bubble of text messages. "He's probably just afraid. You have to push him in the right direction."

I shot her a sideways glance. "You sound like your mother."

Gabby stuck her tongue out at me before admitting, "Well, she isn't always wrong."

Chapter 10

The next day turned out to be especially brutal at work. The new clinic wasn't scheduled to open until the summer, but we wanted to be able to hit the ground running. Which meant, in addition to assessing new clients, I had to sit in on a monthly focus group with our current families finalizing the design of the community areas.

I was sitting in an overly warm room filled with ten parents, fading in and out of the discussion, all the while plotting how to get Matt to agree on a visit. If he wasn't working, I could swing up Saturday, we could hang out for a few hours, *shoot the shit*, as Sean would say and then I'd be home on Sunday to squeeze in some studying. No pressure, no commitment, just...

"Oh, god." Jessica moaned in the seat next to me. "This looks like trouble."

Startled back into reality I looked up and fought back a groan of my own. Despite our informal setting, Marcus had his hand in the air, looking like he was attempting to stop traffic. He and his wife had two kids with celiac disease. They were extremely involved in the development of the clinic and were notorious for coming up with innovations and improvements. Sure enough, Marcus had a stack of drawings laid out in front of him.

My heart sank at the thought.

"Ellen and I were thinking, maybe, you could add some low appliances and countertops to the cooking area, where our kids could test out recipes too." He pointed to a sketch where he had reconfigured a section of the waiting room. "If they take ownership of their meals, they'll be much more likely to eat them, right?"

A great idea, but one that would lead to more design changes. A quick glance at my planner showed we had barely a month before the plumbing and electrical went in. After that, any reconfigurations would be prohibitively expensive. I turned to look at my boss, Jeff, hoping he'd squash the idea immediately.

No such luck.

"I like the concept," Jeff nodded, tapping his finger to his lips. A clear sign he was intrigued. "This is a fairly significant change, but we have a little wiggle room in the budget. Do you all agree this is worthy of the additional time and effort?" He looked around the room and all the parents' heads were bobbing enthusiastically.

"Okay, then." Jeff turned to Jessica and me. "Looks like we need to schedule another meeting with the contractor. Let's get together Saturday to flesh out the plans.

That quickly, my free time this weekend disappeared in a flash. My chest constricted, and a dull throbbing started in one temple.

Work life – 27, Personal life – 0.

Chapter 11

Walking home from class on Friday, I was so busy peering at my texts in the shadowy twilight, I almost got run over by a car leaving the parking garage. Clearly, Matt was becoming a major distraction. I needed to get this pseudo-relationship figured out before I got hurt. Literally. Sure, we'd agreed to take it slow, but I thought that meant strolling in the park, slow, not shifting tectonic plates slow. No point in sabotaging my future if this relationship wasn't going anywhere. Right? I needed to see him soon. In person. Make sure he was as wonderful as I had built him up to be.

As I walked past the Five-and-Ten store on Main Street, there, in the giant plate glass window was the perfect solution. I flew inside, completed a quick transaction, and headed home, whistling a happy tune.

I changed into snuggly PJs covered with rabbits nibbling carrots, spread my books on the table, started dinner, and waited for

Matt's call. I had just tossed the last of the seasonings into my wok and wiped down the counter when my phone buzzed. *Perfect*. I gave the Pad Thai a final stir and pressed Talk. "Hi, handsome."

"Hey, pixie girl. What are you doing?"

"Cooking. Studying. Same old, same old." I tried to keep my voice casual as I ladled the noodles onto a plate and set it next to my stack of textbooks. "How was work? Did you catch any bad guys?"

"No one too terrible. A few speeders, a broken taillight, oh, and an expired registration with about a dozen outstanding parking tickets."

Digging a fork into my dinner, I raised the noodles in salute. "Well, it's a good thing Matt Quinsy's on the job."

"Darn right! How's the nutrition biz?

"Good," I mumbled through the food. "Keeping folks healthy one day at a time. Things are crazy right now, and will only get worse this month, but that's expected."

"Yeah, how come?"

"Halloween's next week...the start of the holiday season. Definitely a horror show for healthy eating. We offer a ton of sessions to coach clients how to make good choices. Which leaves me pretty conflicted, because I love Halloween—chocolate, costumes, drinking. What could be better?"

I heard his dismissive snort through the phone.

"What?"

"I'm not a big fan. Things can get a little wild. You're not going out, are you?" He broke out his stern cop tone, but I was not intimidated.

"Hells, yeah. Midterms will be over next week, so I have a day or two to relax before the end of semester crush." Now was my chance. I took a deep breath and blurted out, "My girls are coming down on Friday to celebrate. Do you wanna join us? You know…as friends. Just doing the "friends" thing."

There was a moment of silence before he said, "Nah, I can't. Gotta work."

Damn. Surely I could tempt him down for one night. I just needed to offer the right incentive. "You may want to rethink that. I have a special costume this year."

"Yeah?" He sounded mildly intrigued.

Meanwhile, I was bouncing in my chair with excitement. "Mmm-hmm. I just bought it today. I think you'll like it." My sing-song tone sounded like an excited five-year-old's.

"Oh yeah, what is it?" I heard his bed squeak as he readjusted himself. I'd definitely caught his interest.

"Picture this. I'm going to be wearing a very short, blue skirt, silver heels, a pair of iridescent wings, and carrying a wand."

"A wand?"

"Of course. What kind of pixie would I be without a wand?"

"A pixie?" The word whooshed out with a kind of crackly sound. Like he'd sat up too quickly and choked a little.

I smiled like a cat who'd trapped a mouse under its paw. "Uh-huh. I remember hearing somewhere that big, handsome New York troopers have a thing for pixies." I twirled the noodles around with my fork, letting the silence build a little. Then I went in for the kill. "Maybe I made a mistake. Maybe it was hot lacrosse players who like them. I'll have to cozy up to my brother's friends and find out for sure."

The answering groan sent an excited prickle down my spine. I suppressed a giggle of delight and notched my final arrow. "I'm glad we're just friends, so it shouldn't bother you when I talk to other guys at the bar." Sliding a small bite of noodles in my mouth, I chewed twice and murmured, "hot guys," through the Pad Thai.

His next sound was an irritated grunt. "You," he growled, "do not fight fair, Lindsay, not Quinsy.

This time, I did laugh. "It comes with having a brother. We spent twenty years trying to best each other." With a shrug, I added smugly, "I usually won."

"Hmm."

He didn't sound impressed. A little cranky, actually. Just as I'd hoped. "So, do you want to reconsider joining me for Halloween? My offer still stands."

This time a heavy sigh surged through the phone. "I wish I could, but I told Jason I'd cover for him. If I had known about your wicked scheme to lure me down there, I might have told him to pound sand."

"Pound sand?"

"Yeah, you know, forget it."

When I didn't respond, he insisted, "It's an expression."

"Uh-huh," and we both laughed.

Then his voice turned low and serious. "Hey, Linds?"

I mimicked his low pitch. "Yeah?"

"Maybe you could send me a picture?"

I chuckled, delighted with his tone. "I guess I could do that."

"Good." There was total silence for one…two…three seconds. And then he softly repeated, "Good."

His sexy baritone sent shivers through me. I had to figure a way to make this work. And soon. Halloween was going to be a bust, but there had to be another option. Ruefully, I stuffed another forkful of noodles in my mouth.

"Where are you going to dazzle the lucky bastards in Delaware?"

I choked as I tried to swallow, surprised but pleased by his jealous tone. "Kilarney's."

"Well, be careful," he growled, "And don't go falling for any lacrosse players or creepy Star Wars characters or anything. I know we said we'd take things slow, but I don't want you hooking up with someone else before I have a chance to show you my patented moves."

Ooow. That sounded promising. I'd love to learn about his moves.

But once we hung up, I nervously gulped down the remainder of my water. *Patented moves?* To be honest, the thought terrified me.

I didn't have moves. My experience was limited to halfhearted fumblings and a handful of unsatisfying gropefests. Hopefully, I wasn't setting myself up for more disappointment.

Chapter 12

Kir and Ash arrived late on Friday.

"Jeez, Main Street is crazy tonight. We're in for a wild time," Kir said as she dropped her overnight bag in my living room.

"Here, we got you this." Ashley thrust an extra-large meat lover's pizza at me and collapsed into my recliner. "Had to fight through a crowd of Oompa Loompas to get the damn thing, but it'll be worth it."

"Thanks. This will make a good base before we go drinking." I pulled out a slice, took a healthy bite and said, in between chewing, "You can trust me on this. I'm a trained professional."

Kir laughed. "I just hope I don't see red sauce resurface all over my car tonight."

"Or on my couch," I added, staring pointedly at Ashley.

"Yeah, yeah. One night of spaghetti and tequila and suddenly I'm the lightweight. Puulease."

I laughed. "I've got extra blankets and pillows for you there in the corner. I had Sean tighten up the frame in the sofa bed, so it shouldn't collapse again tonight."

Walking toward my bedroom, I said, "Make yourselves at home. I'm going to take a shower and get dressed."

I didn't take long to get into my costume. Standing in front of my bedroom mirror, I blinked. *Wow, I really did look like a pixie. An alarmingly erotic pixie.*

Usually, my non-existent breasts, hips and height were a major embarrassment. But by combining a short, frothy, lapis-blue skirt with strappy, silver heels, my legs seemed long and shapely. My wings were an iridescent swirl of purple, turquoise and silver, and the crisscross of blue satin ribbons across my chest made me appear surprisingly voluptuous.

The finishing touch came when Kirsten brushed my short black hair forward and applied sparkly makeup, emphasizing my eyes. They turned a vivid blue and appeared huge—almost otherworldly. A dusting of glitter along my collarbone, and voila, I was a pixie.

"You look amazing," Kirsten whispered.

I could barely take my eyes off my reflection. "*I know*." I giggled, caught between delight and surprise at the transformation.

Damn, I wish Matt was here to see this. The least I could do was send him a picture.

"Thanks. This is great." I gave her a hug and then glanced once again in the mirror. "Can you give me a minute?"

"Sure." She smiled. "No problem. I'll finish getting ready." And she headed into the living room.

Closing the door behind her, I grabbed my phone. The selfie took about five tries, but I finally captured the right look. Matt was going to love this.

Happy Halloween from your favorite pixie. I texted and pressed send.

Excited to hear his response, I bounced on the bed, giggling, waiting.

And...nothing.

I got up, straightened my dresser, put away the makeup.

Still nothing.

I smoothed away the wrinkles on my pink and orange comforter. Fluffed my throw pillows. Checked my phone. There were bars. It was fully charged.

I thought for sure he'd respond. Maybe he was in the shower. Or at work already. Or maybe he wasn't as interested as I'd thought. Damn.

Determined to not let him ruin my evening, I checked the mirror a final time and headed into the living room.

Kirsten and Ashley appeared stunning, as usual. They had draped sheets around themselves, added golden crowns and *ta-da*, they were beautiful Roman goddesses. Simple, elegant and effortless. While that would normally make me jealous, tonight I was more than able to measure up.

"You ready to go?" I asked.

"Absolutely!" Kirsten jumped to her feet and grabbed her keys. I grabbed my wand and we were out the door.

Chapter 13

Kilarney's was unbelievable. Normally it attracted a fairly tame crowd, twenty-something professionals and grad students. But Halloween in Roselle knew no boundaries. There were barely-legal college kids, townies hoping for some action, and even a few professors who had raided their wardrobes and produced some pretty embarrassing outfits from the seventies and eighties.

I was sitting on the end of the largest booth with my buds—Ash and Kirsten, Gabby, Rheannon, Emily, and Kendra—watching the sea of humanity wander past. It felt really good to be hanging with all of them again. Most of them lived in Delaware, but we were all so busy, we didn't find many chances to get together. Tonight felt like old times.

"Want another brain hemorrhage?" Ashley shouted in my ear.

I shook my head. The first three had been delicious, but the combination of Bailey's and schnapps had started to make me queasy.

"I'm going to switch to a beer," I shouted back.

She nodded, clinked glasses with the other girls, and gulped down the floating glob of goo. The drink was really kind of disgusting now that I looked at it.

Needing a change of pace, I grabbed my wand and headed toward the bar. I was bracing myself to worm up to the front of the line when someone grabbed me from behind, enveloping me in an embarrassingly intimate hug. I let out a squeak of surprise. Damn drunken fools.

"Don't crush my wings," I exclaimed and tried to break free. Until I heard his voice.

"God, you look hot."

"Matt?"

"Mmm-hmm," he hummed into my ear.

He came, he came, he came! "What are you doing here? I thought you had to work." Between my excitement and his ridiculously fierce hug, I was barely able to squeeze out the words.

He loosened his grip, allowing me to turn around. "I decided I couldn't miss this. Best decision I have ever made."

"So, you like my costume?"

"You have no idea." His lustful expression made me giggle. Like he was going to strip me naked right there in the bar. While an intriguing thought, we probably needed to spend a little time getting reacquainted. "Sooo, do you want a drink?"

He glanced up, almost surprised to find himself hemmed in by a horde of people. Running a hand through his hair, he sighed, "Yeah, all right. I guess I can do that."

I decided it would be one, very quick drink. Because, damn, the man was pretty drool-worthy in his own right.

He was dressed like a handyman, wearing Duluth work pants and a tool belt. The sleeves of his white thermal shirt were pushed up, giving me a tantalizing view of his muscular forearms. And a stubble of beard emphasized his strong jaw. Oh yeah, here was a handyman who could work on me Any. Day. Of. The. Week.

And twice on Sunday.

He eased his way to the front of the bar and ordered a Coors Lite for me (he remembered!) and a Sam Adams for himself. Handing me my beer, he wrapped his arm around my waist and steered me toward the back room. It was a little less crowded there and we managed to find a high top with two empty stools.

We clinked bottles and took a drink. Excitement and alcohol buzzed through me, making it hard for me to think. *Matt was here.* What did that mean? Was he here as a friend? Would he be willing to be more? Should I play it cool? Because that would be really, really hard for me to pull off in my current state.

I needed answers. Now. I leaned over and shouted into his bicep, "What are you doing here? I thought you had to work."

He offered a half-smile, his eyes pausing at my lips, before running down my legs and back up to my glittery cleavage. Scooting his stool closer, he growled into my ear, "I haven't been able to get you out of my mind. Especially picturing you as a pixie. So, I told Jason he'd have to find someone else to cover."

Hee hee. My plan had worked. I'd never felt so powerful before. I slanted him what I hoped was a coquettish glance. "I sent you a picture."

"Mmm-hmm," he nuzzled into my neck. "I was halfway here when I got it. Almost ran off the road."

Yikes! My pulse accelerated; blood pressure probably running about two hundred over ninety-seven. I might not survive this.

Especially when he added, "Turns out you look even better than I imagined." Lacing his fingers in mine, he brought them up to his lips for a kiss.

Too lightheaded to remain upright, I buried into his chest with a giddy giggle. Sweet Lord, he smelled divine. "I'm glad you came down to see me."

"Hell, I'd drive to Texas to see you like this." Then he pulled back. Tipped up my chin with his index finger and gazed into my eyes. "I'm really glad you invited me. I'll admit, I've been anxious about our relationship—really conflicted." He stroked my cheek. "But I had to see you again."

"I'm glad." My emotions were bubbling too close to the surface. I broke eye contact, afraid he'd read too much into my expression. Grabbing my beer, I took a sip. "How long are you staying?"

His mouth twisted into a pout. "Trying to get rid of me already?"

I slapped his chest with my wand, trying to remain casual. "Hardly. But you said you didn't like Halloween, so I didn't know if you'd made other plans. You know…after you'd said hello to me."

With a scorching look, he said, "Halloween is rapidly becoming my favorite holiday." Then he lowered his head and planted a kiss on me that made my toes curl. Hell, my whole body curled. And pulsed. And quivered with desire like I'd never felt before.

If he kept this up, I would have to jump him in the bathroom stall. Sucking in a breath, I rasped, "I thought we were going to take it slow."

He shifted closer and ran his knuckle along my jawline. "I can do slow." Then he speared his fingers into my hair and dipped his tongue into my mouth where it danced with mine.

Overwhelmed and shaky, I grabbed onto his shoulders. Damn, that man could kiss!

"Get a room, you two!" howled a zombie at a nearby table, slapping his buddy Super Mario on the back. The two began to pantomime a fairly disturbing make-out session, which was remarkably effective at killing the mood.

We had to get out of there. We weren't teenagers looking to make out in a bar. This had the potential to become *something*. I gulped down the rest of my beer and plunked the bottle on the table. "Do you want to go to my apartment? You know…somewhere a little less..." I waved my wand at the other table.

Matt leapt up so quickly, you'd have thought the stool was electrified. "Sure." He drained his bottle, grabbed my hand, and started pulling me toward the door.

His enthusiasm made me laugh. And brought me a moment of sanity. "Hang on. I have to let my friends know I'm going."

I know it was dark in the bar, but I think he may have blushed. "Uh, yeah, right. Sorry. Where are they?"

I pointed to the left with my wand and we weaved our way through the mass of pirates, superheroes and undead. Approaching our booth, I waved. "Hey, girls."

Ashley shifted over to make room for me. "Hey Linds, where you been? We thought you'd ditched us."

Embarrassed and unnerved, I stuttered, "Well, umm, actually, Matt showed up. You know, my cop friend?"

Kirsten hooted with delight. "Really? How cool. Where is he?"

I tugged him forward. "Matt, this is Ashley, Kirsten, Gabby, Emily, Kendra and Rheannon. Everyone, this is Matt."

"Hi Matt," they chorused.

He raised his hand in greeting. "Nice to meet you all."

There was a noticeable lull in the conversation as they gave him an appreciative gaze. Then Rheannon and Emily nudged each other, loudly whispered something wholly inappropriate, and burst out in drunken giggles.

Okay, this could get messy, fast.

I leaned over Ashley and Kirsten. "So, umm, we're gonna get ready to go."

Ashley smirked. "I guess that means you need us to find somewhere else to stay."

I felt myself go red. "If you don't mind."

They laughed. "No, that's fine. I'm sure we can crash somewhere else," Kirsten said.

"We'll need to stop by to get our stuff," Ashley added.

"Okay." I straightened, then leaned back in to whisper, "But don't take too long."

I tried not to flinch as they squealed with excitement. I grabbed Matt's hand and pulled him toward the door.

Chapter 14

Forget butterflies. I was so nervous, it felt like I had pterodactyls flapping around in my stomach. As Matt drove to my apartment, I tried to take deep, calming breaths but it wasn't working. Every nerve ending in my body was tingling with desire, fear, anticipation.

Meanwhile, he was completely composed, eyes on the road, hands at ten and two, idly tapping out a Rush song on the radio.

Maybe he did this kind of thing all the time. Maybe this would be a one-night stand and I'd hate myself in the morning. What then?

I must have made a panicked sound because he turned his head and I could see his smile in the shadows. Feel the warmth in his eyes. And I remembered. He'd driven all the way from New York to see me.

Me.

A pretty big commitment for a one-night stand.

Then we arrived at my apartment and his first words erased all my concerns.

"I'm kind of hungry. You got anything to eat?"

Not exactly a Don Juan seduction. Actually, more like Brad Pitt in *Ocean's Eleven*. That man ate like a Bernese Mountain dog. He's hot and all, but yikes!

The thought put me at ease. I led Matt into the kitchen where he dwarfed my tiny room. "There's not much. I have Ramon noodles, cereal, some Hot Pockets…"

He had the nerve to scoff at me. "I thought you were a nutrition major."

"At the moment, I'm a poor college student. One who doesn't make a habit of inviting large, hungry males to her apartment." I stood there, arms crossed, looking as offended as I could manage.

He crossed his arms to mimic me, but his eyes glinted with humor. "I'm glad to hear it."

I giggled and swatted his arm. "What do you want to eat?"

His dimple popped out. "Cereal's good."

Scooting around, I handed him a bowl and spoon and pointed to the pantry. "Why don't you pick out what you want while I take a shower?"

As I passed, he placed his hand on my arm. "Do you have to?"

I raised my eyebrows and he shrugged. He reached into the pantry and pulled out a box of Raisin Bran. Started to pour it into the bowl before warming me with his gaze. "It's just, I appreciate the costume. I don't think I'm ready for you to take it off." His voice was husky and did crazy things to my insides.

"How about I just go in and freshen up—brush my teeth and stuff?"

He stopped pouring the cereal and stared at me. "That would be nice."

I giggled again. I'd never had a man so fixated on me before. It was a heady feeling. With a flap of my wings, I sashayed into my bathroom. After a few quick swipes with the washcloth, I brushed my teeth and danced back into the kitchen.

Matt was finishing his cereal and his eyes flared when I entered. He stood, picked up the bowl, held it to his lips, and drained the milk, without taking his eyes off me.

God, he was sexy. His eyes were dark, a deep intense brown. Almost black. He still had on the tool belt, which clung to his hips, and his shirt stretched tight across his chest, hinting at an impressive array of muscles. As he carried his bowl to the sink and rinsed it out, I got a nice peek of the back side, too. Strong shoulders, narrow waist, firm ass – I stood there and drank it all in.

When he turned around, he dipped his head in appreciation. "Thanks. That hit the spot. Do you mind if I take a shower? It was pretty hot in the bar."

"Mmmm, sure. Make yourself at home." I enjoyed the view as he picked up his overnight bag and headed into the bedroom. I could not believe I'd invited him here. That we would be taking things to a whole new level— friends with some pretty spectacular benefits. What was I thinking?

Needing to keep busy, I dried Matt's bowl and spoon and returned them to their home. Wiped down the sink. Straightened the chair he'd sat in. Sponged a crumb off the table and rinsed out the sponge.

Wondering what to do next, I headed for the living room, when there was a sharp knock on the front door.

Ashley popped her head in. "Is everybody decent?" I nodded, and she and Kirsten strolled in. "We'll just grab our stuff and be gone." They wasted no time gathering up their clothes and shoving them into their bags.

"Where's your hunk?" Kirsten asked, as she pulled the zipper shut and straightened.

I made a face at her. "In the shower."

At that, he walked out of my bedroom, pausing in the doorway. His hair slicked back, wet. He was wearing a navy blue police academy t-shirt, stretched tight across his chest, soft grey sweatpants low on the hips and no shoes. Barefoot.

My mouth went dry. Sahara Desert dry. I heard Ash make a strange sound. When I pulled my eyes from him, I saw Ash and Kir mesmerized. He was…

There were no words. Hot didn't even begin to describe him. Volcanic, maybe.

"Hi," he said, oblivious to the seismic effect he was having on the room.

"Aaah, hi," they breathed in unison. I shot them a look and it broke the spell.

"Yes, well, we'll be going now. You two have fun." When Kir didn't move, Ashley grabbed her arm, but Kir tugged back.

"Do we have to go? She barely knows him. It's not like they're going to…" she trailed off, glancing at me over her shoulder. Ash handled it in her usual diplomatic fashion, growling at her best friend.

"Stop. I think she might. Let's go." And with a final wave, she propelled Kir out the door.

I fought back a giggle, bubbling up from equal parts embarrassment and nerves.

"They're gone." Master of the obvious, that's me. I smiled and went to lock the door. When I turned back, Matt hadn't moved from the doorway. He was frozen in place. And his brow had a funny little crinkle.

"What?" I crossed over to him.

"That's not why I came here tonight."

It was my turn to stiffen. Had he been serious about the whole friends thing? Because I tell you, I'd definitely changed my mind—a full one hundred and freakin' eighty degrees.

When I offered no response, he shrugged his shoulders and continued, "I mean, I really wasn't thinking about what would happen when I got here. I just wanted to see you. I can't stay long… I have to work tomorrow. I wasn't counting on…I don't want you to think I only came here for…well—" he paused, his eyes worried. "I like you. I don't want you to think this is nothing but a booty call."

One, two, three seconds passed while I let those words sink in. Unable to hold it in any longer, I laughed. Loudly.

"Booty call? You're afraid I might think you drove four hours for a booty call?" I shook my head, trying to get my giggles under control. "And who says that anyway?"

Of course, I had thought the same thing on the drive over, but hearing him offer to wait…well, it told me all I needed to know.

I took a step closer and rested my hands on his delightfully solid biceps. "Trust me. If I didn't want you here, I wouldn't have invited you."

He smiled, and I sighed at the absolute perfection of his face—his eyes crinkled, the dimple popped out of his right cheek and his lips? Well, they were the most kissable things I have ever seen.

Giving him a steady look, I raised up on my toes, leaned a hairbreadth away from his mouth, and whispered, "Get ready, officer, because this pixie plans to make all your adolescent dreams come true."

I could feel the tension drain away. His face lit up and he hollered, "Oh, baby. That's what I wanted to hear!" In a nanosecond, I was crushed in his arms, his lips covering mine.

All the anticipation from the past few weeks exploded into full-fledged desire. My hands roamed up and down his muscular arms, around to his back, locking him in place. Without breaking contact, he walked us back a few steps into the bedroom. God, he smelled divine, like soap and clean cotton and Matt.

Once we were in the room, inches from the bed, he pulled away. In one smooth motion, he crossed his arms at his hips and peeled off his shirt.

I froze. He was absolutely gorgeous. The picture of manliness. And I knew, without a shadow of a doubt, I could not go through with this.

He reached for me and I took a step back, shaking my head. "I changed my mind."

Thinking I was kidding, he went for my arm again. I dodged away.

Realizing I was serious, he raised his hands in surprised surrender. "What do you mean?"

"I can't do this. I mean…look at you."

His hands still raised in the air; he lowered his eyes down his body. "What?"

My gaze followed his and we both stopped when we reached the bulge in his pants.

"Is there something wrong?" He asked, concerned.

"Uhhh, yes," I squeaked, dragging my eyes upward. Then I glanced down at my ridiculously paltry mosquito bites. "Your chest is bigger than mine."

He chuckled, sounding relieved. "Aww, stop," then flexed his pecs, the big jerk. "I spent a ton of time at the gym this month. I've had a lot of nervous energy, thanks to you."

"Even so, you are absolutely gorgeous. You can't want to be with me."

His mouth dropped open. "What are you talking about?"

I swept my hands down in front of me. "Look at me. I'm built like a twelve-year-old boy."

He reared back a little to observe me, slowly, carefully. Then tipping his head to one side, he said with complete sincerity, "I think you're beautiful. I've been fantasizing about you since I pulled you over."

It took all I had not to snort. I stared longingly at his pecs covered in a light dusting of hair, his obliques bracketing impossibly well-defined abs, the happy trail below his navel, disappearing in the waistband of his sweats. Hell, even his belly button was sexy.

Then my gaze returned to his eyes. They were hungry. Craving.

"Seriously?"

He tugged me into his arms, holding me flush against his obviously appreciative body. "Seriously."

Clearly, the man had no sense, but who was I to argue with him. After a month enjoying the most erotic thoughts ever, I'd be crazy to let him slip through my fingers. So, I launched myself at him and we locked lips as though he was my last source of oxygen.

After a few breathless moments, he pulled away, his eyes sparkling. "Whoa, pixie. We have all night. Let's make it last."

Lowering my eyes to his chest, all toned and smooth, I sighed. "I don't know if I can."

He crushed me to him. "Stop that." He ran his hands down my ribs and slowly untied the blue ribbon securing my wings. He slid them off with a swish of satin and let them flutter to the floor. Grabbing my hips, he eased his thumbs between my skirt and shirt. Burning a trail of heat, he slid my top up and over my head. Standing there in my little lacy bra, I went warm under his intense gaze.

"Oh, yes. This was definitely worth the trip," he whispered. "You are beautiful. Perfect."

I blushed. "Stop."

"No. Come here." He wrapped his arms around me and pressed me against his hard body. Very hard body. His hands slid down to my butt and squeezed while his lips covered mine.

I stroked his muscular back and then trailed up, lacing my fingers around his neck. He nuzzled my ear and in the sexiest tone asked, "Are you sure you want to do this?"

Chapter 15

Was I sure? Hell, I'd never been so certain.

When I nodded, he let out a whoop, picked me up, and tipped backward onto the bed. We fell onto the mattress in a jumble of arms and legs, feverishly groping each other. I knocked throw pillows onto the floor while he dragged down the covers beneath us. When he tucked my body under his and slowly lowered his lips to mine, I could feel his heat surrounding me. He thrust his tongue in my mouth—strong and dominant. I pictured it probing my most intimate areas. *Oh, this was going to be good.*

He locked eyes with me and the smile that slid over his face was so sexy, I almost came on the spot. Eagerly, I slid his sweats from his hips and groped his bare butt.

Oh, God. It was as firm as I'd imagined. Total perfection. The feel of his skin made me so hot and wet, I could hardly lay still.

Mirroring my movements, he eased his hand up my thigh, under my skirt, and gave my right cheek a squeeze. When his other hand tried to join the action, my crumpled skirt got in the way. Without taking his lips from mine, he slid the offending garment down my legs, leaving me in nothing but my matching teal bra and panties and silver heels.

Only then did he pull away from me. And the look he gave me...I was beautiful.

With an eager growl, he sank back into the mattress and kissed me deeply, fiercely. Getting his fill, he began to trail his lips across my cheek, jaw, and down to my collarbone. His thumb stroked me through the lacy fabric of my bra before tugging down the cup and caressing my sensitive peak.

We both moaned in pleasure.

Using the pad of his thumb, he brushed my nipple lightly at first and then with increasing pressure as it tightened. When he gently pinched the hardened bud, little electrical shocks shot down my belly. I arched my back, pressing my head into the pillow and groaned. Low and deep. Like an animal.

Digging my fingers into his shoulders, I held him in place, silently begging him to continue this blissful torment.

Which he did. He rolled my sensitive skin carefully between his fingers, before gently tugging it, longer, harder. Then he slid his hand over to the right side. I peeked through my lashes to watch him repeat the process, his eyes hooded, his jaw tightened in concentration as he focused intently on his thumbs' ministrations.

A smile curled the corner of his mouth when I let out another moan. He pinched and tugged until I was squirming with need. And then slowly, tantalizingly, he lowered his head and sucked it into his mouth.

I almost bucked off the bed. Raking my fingers through his hair, I pressed him to me. "Oh God, don't stop. That feels incredible."

A sexy chuckle rumbled through his chest. "Not to brag, but I think I can make it better."

He flicked open my bra and his large hand covered my breast, enveloping it in warmth. His soft, hot lips laved one side and then the other. Past boyfriends rarely offered more than a moment's attention to my paltry excuse for a bosom, before moving down to their primary target. But Matt was dedicating a well-appreciated amount of time, and I found myself teetering on the brink.

I kept him pressed tightly to me, running my hands through his soft, brown hair, digging my nails into his neck; the sensations too delightfully, unbearably strong. He didn't seem to mind, continuing to lick and suck my flushed skin, like a cat with a bowl of cream.

After worshiping my breasts, he pulled out from my grasp and continued downward, across my ribs, stomach, dipping his tongue into my belly button before stopping at my one remaining scrap of blue silk.

I quivered as his fingers hooked the sides of my panties and pulled them slowly, seductively, agonizingly down my legs, past my knees, and over my feet. Then he slipped off my shoes and tossed them onto the floor with the rest of my costume.

There. I was naked. That had always made me embarrassed, but tonight I was magnificent. Alluring. And desperate.

"Don't stop now," I whispered.

His smile widened. "Yes, ma'am."

Sliding his own pants off, he afforded me only the briefest glimpse of his magnificence before kneeling next to the bed. He lowered his head to run his tongue around my navel. His hands rested on my knees, but as his mouth sank lower, his palms rose upwards, warming my thighs. His fingers splayed across my skin before skimming the spot where I wanted him most. My heart pounded erratically as I waited.

At the first touch, I groaned.

At the second brush, I moaned.

And when he finally put his tongue on me and licked, I actually screamed. "Oh God, yes!" I wrapped my legs around his torso and locked him into place.

I risked a glance down and found myself pinned by black eyes, intense, hungry. Keeping his gaze locked with mine, he licked my center with a firm and deliberate caress.

It was beyond hot. The sensation was so erotic, I had to close my eyes and just let it ripple over me.

He shifted to run a finger inside while his tongue continued to tease. It only took a few seconds before I came with a scream. He continued to stroke me as the shudders wracked my body. I swear, it had never, ever felt like that before.

Finally, I dropped my legs off his shoulders and collapsed.

Matt drew up next to me. I cracked an eyelid and noticed he appeared very pleased with himself. As well he should.

"Did you have a good time?"

Feeling boneless and a little embarrassed, I closed my eyes and nodded.

"Good." His voice was husky and needy. His finger skimmed across my jaw and down my throat. After brushing my collar bone, it trailed over my chest and slowly, softly circled my nipple. "You're not falling asleep on me, are you?"

I peeked out from under my lashes. The glint in his eye gave no doubt as to his intention. His body, hot and hard, pressed against mine.

Ah yes. There was more, wasn't there? How wonderful.

I smiled at the thought and was delighted by his answering grin. *Oh, this was going to be good. Real good.* I should definitely stay awake for this.

His lips met mine and I could taste his hunger. Feel the intensity of his desire. And my brain fell into a lazy, hazy fog.

His hand settled on my hip, stroking, caressing. Then it moved to my back, down to my bottom where he tugged me closer.

His breath hitched as I rotated my hips against his arousal. Enjoying the sensation, I wrapped my arm around his back and gyrated in a slow, steady dance. *Damn, it felt amazing.*

Matt groaned and pressed me onto my back. Then he raised up and cupped my face, asking softly, "Are you ready?"

That stirred a moment of rationality. Propping up onto my elbows, I stammered, "Wait. So, do you have…umm…you know…any…"

"Any what?" he asked, a twinkle in his eye. "Any breath mints? Cheese curls?"

I slapped his shoulder and he winced in mock pain. Then leaned over the side of the bed and pulled a long ribbon of condoms from his sports bag. "Do you mean these?"

I gasped at the obvious amount of preparedness. Narrowing my eyes, I said, "I thought you said you weren't planning anything tonight."

"I said I wasn't *counting* on it. That doesn't mean I wasn't hoping." He tried to look innocent, with little success. "But if you don't want to, I can just—" He sat up and swung his legs off the bed.

I lunged for him, wrestling him down onto his back. "Don't even *think* about leaving this bed," I growled.

He strained forward to kiss me, but I had him pinned down. Feeling the corded muscles under my hands, I knew he could easily break away, but instead he flopped back into the pillows and awaited my next move.

The blaze in his eyes made me light up from inside. What a delicious opportunity. The man was a walking fantasy.

Straddling his hips, I took control. I stroked his arms, slowly, softly, absorbing the feel of each hill and valley. I traced a small tattoo on his shoulder then kneaded his deltoids, biceps, triceps. Once I'd memorized that area, I moved on to his chest. I ran my fingers through his hair, lightly scratching the skin underneath. As I got closer to his copper-colored nipples, he flexed his pecs. Very nice.

He remained still until I ran my fingertips over his nipple. Then he growled, bucking his thighs eagerly against my buttocks.

I shifted my weight backward until I was rubbing against his impressive appendage and he groaned deep and long. I locked eyes with his and flashed him a wicked, sultry smile. God, I had never felt so powerful. So erotic. It turned me on more than I thought possible.

"Are you ready," I purred.

The look he shot me was electrifying. "Yes."

"Are you sure?" I smiled, mirroring the question he'd asked me earlier.

His response was instantaneous. He flipped me over and bracketed me with his arms. "There is nothing in this universe I am more sure of." He grabbed a foil packet, ripped it open with his teeth, and quickly rolled it in place. With a fierce, demanding kiss, he settled over me and guided himself in.

Oh, baby! He was thick and perfect. And so ready.

Setting a steady rhythm, he slid in and out, in and out, teasing, taunting. Shifting to rest his weight on one arm, his free hand took possession of my breast, pinching it, scraping it with his nails, sending shivers down my spine. All the while kissing me as though wanting to swallow me whole. His blatant desire was intoxicating. And arousing beyond measure.

Barely able to draw a breath, I survived on gasps and pants, which he swallowed with each kiss. Determined to kill me with pleasure, he slid his hand down my chest and reached between us, where we were joined. His fingers rubbing, circling, pressing into my aching folds.

His eyes were tightly closed, jaw set, reining in his climax. The pressure began to build as he stroked my tingling center, harder. Harder. Oh yes! He was going to take me with him. I clutched his shoulders, tightly bunched with exertion, and let the sensations take over.

"Yes. Yes! Don't stop," I keened, thrusting up to meet him. Hearing me moan through our joined lips, he increased his pace. The pleasure built and built until it finally burst into sparks along every nerve ending in my body. With a roar, Matt followed. Then he collapsed on top of me, flattening all the air out of my lungs.

I lay there, encompassed by the scent, the feel, of a warm, happy male.

"Sorry," he murmured. "I'll try to move. Just give me a second."

Smiling at the completely sated tone of his voice, I ran my hands over his back, enjoying the slick texture of his skin. "I'm fine. Stay right here. I don't want you to go."

"Mmm." He kissed my ear. "Don't worry, pixie girl. I'm not going anywhere."

Chapter 16

The next morning, I woke up to Matt's warm body wrapped around mine. My foofy pink and orange comforter was in a crumpled heap on the floor. Sunlight streaming through the window glinted on my wand, throwing rainbow sparkles across the ceiling. I hummed contentedly. It felt like we'd been transported into fairyland.

"Good morning." Matt nuzzled into my neck.

"Good morning to you, too." I turned within the circle of his arms and kissed his scratchy cheek. His dimple popped out. Delightful.

Blinking a few times, he yawned and gave an enormous stretch, his feet untucking the sheets at the bottom of the bed. Then he pulled me back down on his chest and slid his hand behind his head. His bulging bicep drew my attention, where I became distracted by the tattoo on his shoulder. I'd noticed it last night but had other far more pressing things on my mind at the time.

I reached up and traced four little numbers. "What do these mean?"

He kissed my head. "That's my badge number. I got it when I joined the force."

I loved the way his voice grumbled in his chest. "Hmmm." I snuggled deeper.

"Hmmm what?" he asked, suddenly intent.

I shook my head and continued tracing.

He grabbed my hand and pressed it flat. "Pix? Do you mind me being a cop?"

I looked up at his stubbly jaw "Mind? Like does it scare me or something?" I grimaced. "A little. But it's not like you're going to get hurt handing out tickets, right?"

With a flinch, he grumbled, "There's a little more to my job than that. I've been in a few hairy situations over the years. But that's not what I meant."

"Then what *are* you asking?"

He pressed my head to his chest and squeezed. "Like, umm, if we started dating…would it be enough for you?"

His voice sounded so vulnerable, I wiggled up to a seated position, ignoring the *whole if we started dating* comment, and asked, "What do you mean, is it enough?"

"Well," he started, staring across the room, "my last girlfriend—" He glanced up at me with a wan smile and shrugged. "Never mind. It doesn't matter."

"Yes, it does." I stuffed pillows behind my back and pulled him over to lie on my chest. "Who was this idiot girlfriend and what did she say to you?"

He ran a hand over his stubble and then through his hair, clearly uncomfortable he'd brought this up. But I wasn't about to let him off the hook. "Come on. Out with it."

He groaned. "Her name was Rachel and she was from Long Island. A fashion major. We met junior year."

I hated her already. "And?"

He stroked the satiny pink strip edging my blanket for a moment, before flicking it away in disgust. "*And* I fell head over heels. We practically lived together our last year in school. I couldn't get enough of her. I thought we'd get married once we graduated, but..." His voice trailed off.

My heart lodged in my throat. Maybe this was what had scarred him…why he was so hesitant to date me. "But what? What happened?" I prodded.

The blanket made a swishing sound as he pulled the satin back and forth between his fingers. "Well, when we graduated, her father got her a job in New York City. And a brownstone in Brooklyn." His voice was strained now. Gruff. "She wanted me to move there and help her renovate it. She thought I could get over the 'cop thing' and make some real money in real estate. I'd do the grunt work, she'd decorate it and then we'd flip it. 'Easy money,' she'd said."

"Huh. How special of little miss Rachel to have everything planned out for you." I did my best not to growl.

He squinted at me with a wry twist of his lips. "Yeah. I guess." He lay his head back down on my chest. His hair was short and soft and it tickled a little, but I didn't mind. I liked the feel of his weight on me.

He was not as comfortable. He cocked his head till his neck cracked, then settled back down. "I was living in Albany at the time, trying to get on the force. I'd drive down to the City to see her on weekends. All she wanted to do was go to clubs, but I wasn't really into the whole partying thing. And she kept pushing me to help renovate her house."

"I have to admit, you did look pretty hot in a tool belt tonight."

He laughed, as I'd hoped, and pressed a kiss on my knuckles. "Thank you."

"No, thank *you*," I drawled, praying he'd continue. After running an agitated hand through his hair, he did.

"After about a year, I finally heard from the NYSP. I got in, obviously. But when I told Rachel the good news—that was it—she dumped me. She said she still loved me, and if I would have changed my mind about becoming an officer, we could've gotten married. But since I was going to go through with it..."

"What? How horrible! She dumped you over your career choice?" I squeezed him hard enough, he grunted.

Rubbing his lips over my collarbone, he mumbled into my skin, "I found out later she was actually seeing someone else. A coworker. I guess *he* had the right kind of job." He stared up at me with a grimace of pain. "See, in college, it seemed like we'd wanted the same things, but once we were apart, Rachel changed so much." His voice dropped to a whisper. "I wasn't enough anymore. That's when I realized long-distance relationships couldn't work."

I hardly knew what to say. My chest hurt thinking about it. "I'm so sorry, Matt."

With a flick of his hand, he attempted to brush away my concern. "It turned out for the best. Soon after I got out of the Academy, my dad found out he had systolic heart failure, and I moved back home." His voice roughened, and he flopped onto his back. "She definitely would not have approved of that."

I propped up on my elbow. "Is your dad okay now?" Having worked with people affected by cardiovascular disease, I knew he could be in bad shape.

"Yeah. Things were pretty touch and go for a while, but he got a transplant about three years ago." His fingers trailed up and down my arm, more of an unconscious gesture than a caress. "I still worry about him. He doesn't always do what the doctor says. When I remind him, he gets all moody. Then mom tells me to leave him alone. It becomes a whole big thing."

Clearly, Matt did not like to have his wishes disregarded. I rested my palm on his shoulder, kneaded the taut muscles under his silky skin and asked, soothingly, "What doesn't he do?"

The muscles bunched tighter. "He should eat better. But mom doesn't like to see him suffer. I can't tell you the number of times I've caught her baking him cookies or sneaking bacon on his sandwiches.

Bacon!" He shook his head in disgust. "Don't even get me started on his lack of cardio. He says he gets enough exercise cutting grass and shoveling snow...the two things he's been told not to do." He sighed. "It's just frustrating."

I ran a soothing hand across his back. "I can certainly sympathize. Many of my patients have a hard time accepting the limitations on their lifestyle. Would you like me to talk to him?"

"No, that's all right. I just need to convince him to listen to the doctors. He'll come around eventually."

I wasn't so sure, but maybe he was right. He could be very convincing when he wanted to be.

Determined to change the subject into a more enjoyable direction, I wrapped my arms around him in a bear hug, "Well, it may sound petty, but I'm glad Rachel didn't appreciate you because I think you're wonderful." I poked his tattoo. "Even if you are a cop."

He grunted and grabbed my ribs, tickling me.

Giggling, I twisted away and pinned him under me. Then leaning in real close, I whispered, "Do you want to know my favorite thing about police officers?"

He raised his eyebrows, concern replaced by a lazy grin of anticipation.

"Those Miranda rights." Wiggling my hips against him, I purred, "Especially the part about 'whatever I say can and will be held against me.'"

Chapter 17

We stayed in bed most of the day, finally emerging mid-afternoon to grab provisions from the kitchen.

I marveled at Matt's graceful movements as he prowled around for food. He was extraordinarily sexy in his grey sweatpants and nothing else.

Finding nothing but vegetables in the fridge, he pried a box of Hot Pockets and a pizza from my freezer. I reached around him to turn on the oven for the pizza while he heated up the ham and cheese croissants in the microwave.

Once the microwave dinged, he put the plates on the table, poured us each a glass of milk, and sat down. I took a few small bites of the Hot Pocket and put the remainder back on the plate. He quickly polished off his portion and pointed at my piece. When I pushed the plate towards him and he downed that too, as well as the glass of milk. I could see I was going to have to stock up better on groceries if he was going to visit again.

Content for the moment, he took my hand in his. Hair tousled, light stubble on his jaw, and eyes amber in the sunlight, he looked like a contented lion. *Rrowww*. I could get very used to this.

Then he had to go and ruin it with a cold dose of reality. Glancing up at the clock, he said, "I have to head back soon."

I grimaced then kissed his knuckles. "I know."

"I had fun," he smiled, running his fingertips up and down my arm.

"I did too." It tickled, so I batted him away.

Not easily deterred, he moved his hand to my bare thigh, peeking out below the hem of his blue police academy t-shirt. "I'd like to do this again sometime."

I waggled my eyebrows. "Shouldn't we eat the pizza first?"

He laughed, his eyes soft and warm. "I meant see you again. Maybe next time, you'll take me on a real date, so I don't feel so cheap."

Next time. My heart trip hammered at the words. "Does this mean we are going to violate your 'no long-distance dating' rule?"

He looped his arms around my hips and pulled me onto his lap. "I think we just did."

Sure, sort of. But I needed to make sure. Because I was falling fast and wanted to know we were on the same page. "Seriously, Matt, are you okay with us dating? Can you handle this after the whole Rachel thing?"

His mouth pressed flat and he stared into my eyes like he wanted to probe my soul. My stomach, which had a jittery flutter, turned full-on cyclone.

Looking away, he said gruffly, "I'll be honest. I don't know."

Ouch! I must have squeaked in pain because he quickly refocused and pressed his large, warm palm to my cheek.

"Sorry, Linds, but that's the truth. I really like you. But it may not be enough. In fact, it could make this harder." He dropped his head to my shoulder, nuzzled his nose into my neck. He puffed out a breath, tickling my collarbone.

I stiffened, afraid to move. Afraid what his next words would be.

He raised his head and our eyes locked. His face softened. "I tell you what. I can give it a try. I think we can make it work. As long as you promise not to change and find fault with everything about me."

The queasy turmoil inside settled a little. "I think I can manage that." I leaned back to nibble his earlobe and whispered, "I think you're pretty perfect, just the way you are."

A slow grin slid up his face and that irresistible dimple popped out. "I think you're pretty perfect too." Rubbing his nose against mine, he asked hesitantly, "When do you think we can get together again?"

Hot damn! He really was interested. Eagerly, I glanced at the refrigerator. And my heart pinched. Sliding off his lap into my own chair, I motioned toward the calendar hanging on the door. Almost every block contained a dizzying array of colors—pink for class, orange for work, blue for meetings. There was no relief until the end of November, where five days were relatively color-free. "Thanksgiving's coming up. I could drive up for a few days, maybe meet your family?"

At his sudden frown, I backpedaled, "Or not. Sorry, it's obviously way too soon to do the whole family thing."

"No, that's not it." He leaned back in his chair, raking his fingers through his hair. "It's just, Thanksgiving is the busiest travel time of the year. I'll be working six 10s that week."

"Huh?"

"Sorry. Six ten-hour days."

Damn. "But I don't have school all week."

He grimaced. "Sorry, but I won't have much time off and when I do, I'll be on call. It won't work." Noticing my disappointment, he quickly said, "I'll have some time off in early December."

Now it was my turn to be a killjoy. Red marks on the calendar meant exams and deadlines. The first two weeks of the month were like a bloodbath. Afraid to look at him, I started brushing crumbs into a little pile before sweeping them onto my empty plate. "I've got finals coming up and I have to focus on my thesis. I'm going to be slammed until mid-December."

He huffed out a breath. "And now you know why long-distance relationships don't work." The smile on his lips didn't reach his eyes.

Chapter 18

As soon as I'd helped cleaning up Thanksgiving dinner, I raced in the living room to give Matt a call. It had been twenty-six days since I'd seen him last. I was seriously bummed we couldn't spend the holiday together. Or any days, for that matter.

He picked up on the fourth ring, barked, "Hang on," then dropped the phone and exclaimed, "Mom, put that down! I said I'd get it for you." There were a few moments of muffled sounds before Matt moaned, "Mom, I can't believe you made creamed onions. You know he shouldn't be eating that." Then more mumbling. It sounded like a whole lot of drama going on in Albany. Poor Matt.

My day had been very pleasant. Our whole family pitched in to prepare our favorite dishes before sitting down to eat and drink and share treasured memories of past years together. Gran had flown in from Vegas, where she'd moved after grampy died. *Vegas!* Apparently, only "old people" moved to Florida and she still had plenty of life left in her.

She'd brought her boyfriend, Carlos with her. He'd kept us in stitches regaling us about his days as a bellhop at The Flamingo. The six of us talked ourselves hoarse and ate ourselves into a near-coma state.

I stretched out on my parent's sofa and had just started to doze off when I heard Matt holler, "Okay. You do whatever you want. I'm going to talk to Lindsay now." I cracked my eyes open and scooted upright.

"Hey. Happy Thanksgiving," he said, gruffly.

"Thanks. Same to you. Trouble at home?"

He groaned, frustration clearly bleeding through the phone. "You're a dietician. Tell me, is it really a good idea for a man with heart disease to eat creamed onions? And sweet potatoes with an oil spill of butter on top?"

I opened my mouth to answer, but it must have been a rhetorical question because he barreled on. "And my mom. I told her I'd help out. She shouldn't have to do everything herself. But no, she's lugging around an eighteen-pound turkey and peeling five pounds of potatoes, like she's feeding an army. What's with them?"

This time he took a breath long enough for me to respond. "It sounds like you have your hands full up there."

"Yeah, I guess. But really, it's fine. They're family. How are things going at your house?"

I rubbed my overstuffed belly, sighing with contentment. "Great. Dinner was delicious. I ate way too much. Grans kept talking to me about my work and asking how many calories everything had. She's worried about her weight—at eighty-two! Then Carlos chimed in, asking which food was the strongest aphrodisiac. When I told him the oyster stuffing, he winked at me every time he took a bite."

"Who the hell is Carlos?"

His jealous tone made me giggle. "Calm down. He's my Grans' seventy-eight-year-old boyfriend. He's about five-six and looks like a garden gnome."

His disgruntled harrumphing tickled my ear from two hundred miles away. "You're certainly in a mood today." I stretched out and tucked a pillow under my head.

"Well, I've worked a week's worth of hours already and it's only Thursday. People driving like they're the only ones on the road, crashing into each other, rolling cars down embankments. It's nuts. Then I finally get a day off, and nobody's doing what they're supposed to. And then you call, all giddy about how much fun you're having with Carlos and oysters, and it rubbed me wrong. I feel like I'm shouldering all the responsibility and you're down in Delaware without a care in the world."

Seriously? That comment pricked my pride. "Hey! You're not the only one with responsibilities, you know. I'm working just as hard as you are."

"Oh really? How many bodies did you have to scrape off the pavement this week?"

Ouch, that was a pretty low blow. Without thought, I lashed out. "Well, I didn't choose to be a cop. If you don't like it, maybe you should get a new job!"

The silence on the other end was pained and profound. My stomach, full of turkey dinner, flipped like a breaching whale. I'd sounded like Rachel. Not intentionally, but... "Matt, I was—"

"And there it is." His voice, an arctic blast, cut me off.

My throat constricted. "You know I didn't mean that." I choked out.

"No," he growled, "it's fine. I should have known better."

"No!" I moaned, desperately wishing I could take it back. "You know that's not what I was saying. You were acting all high and mighty like your career was more important than mine and I got angry."

"Uh, huh. Well, I'm angry, too. And pretty damned disappointed." His voice cracked a little. "Have a nice Thanksgiving." And he hung up.

Damn. Damn, damn, damity damn it to hell! I banged the back of my head against the back of the sofa with each curse. How could I have said such a thing? And why did he have to interpret it as though I was condemning his job? I truly wasn't.

I slumped into the cushions with a groan. I'd have to call him back. But he was having such a shitty day, he probably wouldn't answer. I should wait a few hours, let him calm down and hopefully gain some perspective. Needing a distraction until then, I dragged myself into the den to watch football with the family.

Chapter 19

It took two phone calls, four texts and a Facetime chat before we got things worked out. As happy as we were when together, being apart was really a strain. Matt was right—long-distance relationships sucked big-time.

Luckily, we got through it and Matt surprised me with a visit the following Wednesday. Despite my jammed schedule and desperate need to study, we had a lovely thirty-six hours together.

My parents were eager to meet the man who took my mind off working non-stop, so they invited us over for dinner. It felt oddly comfortable to have Matt sitting at my dining room table talking with my family. I could almost picture us celebrating the holidays together for the next sixty years.

"Your folks are really nice," he said later that night as we curled up in front of the TV in my apartment.

"Thanks. I think they liked you too. Did you get enough to eat? I could fix you something."

He groaned, patting his stomach, "No, I'm stuffed! Those chicken and dumplings were delicious."

I curled up in his arms, enjoying his warmth. "I'm glad. My dad loves to cook and he would be crushed if you didn't appreciate his efforts."

"Yeah, my mom's the same way."

He stroked my arm and I burrowed deeper. "So, what are your parents like, other than hard-headed rule-breakers who don't listen to their son's well-intentioned advice?"

He snorted. "They're not that bad. Mom's a sweetheart. She loved to spoil us kids, baking cookies, driving us to sporting events, helping out at school—typical mom. Now that we're grown, she spoils my dad instead.

"And what's he like?"

"Well, nowadays he spends most of his time reading the paper and arguing with the TV. But when I was growing up, he worked, came home, puttered around the house. He'd occasionally do stuff with us kids—throw a baseball or take us camping—but mainly he'd just yell at us to pipe down."

I kissed the top button on his soft, grey flannel and said, "That's totally opposite from my life. My mom has a Ph.D. and works as a director for a pharmaceutical company. I get my drive to achieve from her. My dad's more laid back. He's a freelance writer and worked from home. Which meant he was the one to cook, clean house, take us to practices and stuff."

"And your dad was okay with that?"

I pulled back at the weird tone in his voice. "Uh, okay with what?"

"You know, being stuck at home with the kids."

He had a crease between his eyes. Judging. I didn't like it. "I don't think he viewed it as being stuck."

"You know what I mean. Shouldn't your mom have done more to help out?"

A prickle of concern danced down my spine. "Doing what? He was an awesome dad and probably did a better job at home than my mom could have."

When Matt raised his eyebrows. I poked him in the stomach. "Didn't you enjoy dinner tonight? Said they were the best dumplings you'd ever had? If my mom had cooked, you would have gotten one of two options. Winter is soup and sandwiches, summer is a fruit plate."

"I'm sure she could do better than that."

"Maybe, but she didn't want to. She was happy working."

"And your dad didn't resent it? Her job taking precedence over his." Matt pulled himself upright and drew his ankle over his knee. Now we weren't touching.

I didn't like the way this was going. I grabbed a pillow and hugged it to my chest. "You've got it wrong. He's proud of her. She is the director of regulatory safety. Her group makes sure drug therapies meet protocols before they go to market. Pretty important stuff."

"And his work wasn't?"

"What? No, I mean, yes. You don't understand. His work was important. And he loved being at home. Mom knew he was doing a great job taking care of us, so, it worked."

He shrugged. "I don't know…it sounds a little too hippy-dippy for me."

"Hippy dippy?" I swatted him with the pillow, sort of playful, but mainly irritated. His attitude was making me nervous. We hadn't talked about a long-term commitment or anything, but if things progressed…

He must have realized he'd crossed a line because his face grew somber. "I'm sorry, Pix. Let's not fight. Whatever they did is fine by me; because you turned out perfect." He kissed me softly on the lips, and when he pulled back, his dimple was on full display. Just like that, my sexy Matt was back.

Chapter 20

The next day, I took Matt to class with me, where he patiently listened to a fascinating lecture on the dietary ramifications of glucose intolerance. Then we returned to my room where he demonstrated an amazingly diligent ability to distract me while I tried to study for my therapies final. Luckily, I was acing the class, so I didn't put up much of a fight.

Once we took care of *that* particular issue, I whipped up some grilled cheese and tomato sandwiches for lunch.

"When's your Christmas break start?" Matt asked, watching me slide a third sandwich onto his plate.

I glanced at the calendar on my fridge. December appeared to be a lot less colorful in the second half. "I'm done on the sixteenth. Why?"

"I really want to spend more time with you. I was thinking maybe we could go away together. My brother has a nice little place in Vermont. We could go up there, ski, relax, forget all about work and school and everything."

I couldn't resist tweaking him. "Like a real couple? That would be awesome."

He swatted my butt. "Cut it out. We are a real couple."

I dropped into his lap and nuzzled his neck. "Well, I'm glad to hear it. I wouldn't go on vacation with just anyone." I trailed my finger down his nose. "Although I don't know how to ski."

He grabbed my finger and kissed the tip. "Don't worry. I'll teach you."

Sweet! I was going to have my own personal, sexy ski instructor.

He popped half the sandwich into his mouth. Downing the rest of his milk, he continued. "I can get off for a few days before the holiday. How about you drive up on the seventeenth, meet my parents, and then we can head over to Vermont. We can stay through the twenty-first."

"So, we'd have four whole days together?"

His dimple peeped out. "Yup. Sound good?"

"It sounds perfect!" Throwing my arms around him, I planted an enthusiastic kiss on his beautiful lips.

Scooting back his chair, he picked me up and swung me around, my legs dangling in the air. "Good. I'll call my brother when I get home and make sure it's okay."

"Perfect. Now get out of here, so I can study."

***

The next few weeks were a bear. I'd drag myself out of bed, grab an everything bagel and a venti dark with an extra shot on the way to class, then head to the library. If I was lucky, I could squeeze in a sandwich on my way to work, before counseling patients how to remain healthy over the holidays. The irony of that did not escape me.

After fighting through rush hour, I'd return home, whip up a quick salad or stir fry, and study until midnight. Matt was being seriously neglected and he was a kind of grumpy about it, but we made do with texts and FaceTime.

Despite the challenge, I was thrilled he'd gotten over his reticence over long-distance dating and had embraced our budding relationship.

Chapter 21

Finally, my exams were done and the seventeenth arrived. I drove up to Matt's house, nervous and excited. Four days with him seemed like a luxury, so I was surprised at how anxious I felt. There wasn't anyone else I'd rather be with, but this seemed like a big step.

I pulled up into his driveway and Matt came bounding out of the house. When he dragged me out of my seat and gave me a scorching kiss, all my worries disappeared.

"I missed you," he growled into my hair.

I smiled into his neck. "I can tell. I missed you too."

When we pulled apart, the cold hit me. The temperature must have dropped about twenty degrees since I'd left Delaware. Seeing me shiver, Matt grabbed my hand and we ran inside.

Sitting in the living room was an older man in a shapeless taupe sweater and khakis reading a newspaper.

"Hey, Dad, I'd like you to meet Lindsay. Lindsay, this is my dad, Phil."

He glanced up from his paper and peered at me over his half-glasses. "So, you're Matt's girlfriend."

"Yes, sir," I nodded, giving him a quick assessment. He was alert, color was good, weight seemed appropriate, no obvious signs of cardiovascular distress. I wasn't able to conduct a more thorough evaluation because our conversation came to an abrupt end as Phil called out, "Marge! Get in here. Matt's girlfriend is here," and returned his attention to the paper.

I glanced at Matt and he grimaced, as if to say, *that's my dad.*

His mom came bustling in from the kitchen, wiping her hands on a towel. She was plump and pretty with Matt's kind brown eyes and a wide, friendly smile. Oh, and the same sweet dimple right there on her cheek.

"Welcome to our home!" she cried and enveloped me in a hug. Stepping back, she gave me a once-over and announced, "Oh, aren't you a pretty thing. Phil, look at her. Isn't she sweet?"

He gave me a cursory glance and said gruffly, "She looks like those damn fairies you've got all over the place."

"Pixies, dear. They're pixies." She smiled at me. "I collect them. They are ever so cute, don't you think? I can't get enough of them."

Matt squeezed my hand and we shared a secret smile.

"Why don't you come into the kitchen? I've made you some snacks for the trip."

Snacks, how cute. I loved his mom already. We walked in to find sandwiches, fruit, homemade cookies…and about four hundred pixies. They were stuck to the fridge, perched on window ledges, hanging from wind chimes—and every damn one of them had enormous blue eyes, a turned-up little nose, and a skirt short enough to arouse a dead man.

I didn't risk a glance at Matt for fear I would burst out laughing. This truly must have been torture for a young man. I couldn't resist adding to his misery. Putting my elbows on the kitchen island, I rested my chin in my palms and made my butt stick out. "Is there anything I can do to help, Mrs. Quinsy?"

"Oh, no dear. I'm almost done. Let me just pack everything up into a cooler for you." And she fluttered toward an oversized pantry larger than my bedroom.

As soon as her back was turned, I wiggled my ass at Matt. He growled and gave me a quick swat before his mother returned.

"Here you go." She waved a brightly-colored insulated bag at us before tucking the food and utensils into the compartments. "I know it's not a long trip, but this way you'll have something to eat when you get there. Mattie's always hungry and this will tide you over till you get to the grocery store." She winked at me. "We don't want him to be cranky, do we?"

Mattie? That was hysterical. I would never have thought my giant, imposing boyfriend would have a nickname like Mattie. Or that his mom would talk about him like a three-year-old. I loved it!

Apparently, *Mattie* did not. He strode forward and grabbed the bag off the island. "I'm standing right here, Mom. And I don't get cranky."

Which was funny, because he certainly sounded cranky. I glanced at his mom and she sent me a knowing look. But she reached up to pat his face. "I'm sorry, dear, you're right. I was being mean. I simply want to make sure you both have a nice trip."

He leaned over to kiss her cheek. "I know. Thanks, this is great. We're going to get going now, okay?"

"Oh, yes, you two have fun."

"Thanks, Mrs. Quinsy. It was lovely meeting you."

"Call me Marge, dear. And it was a pleasure to meet you, too."

We walked out through the living room where Marge gave us both hugs and Phil nodded from behind his paper.

Outside, we pulled my bags out of my car and quickly packed them into Matt's truck, because, *damn*, it was cold!

He slammed the tailgate shut. "Well, Pix, you ready to go?"

I nodded. If I was a puppy, I'd have wagged my tail. Maybe even piddled a little.

Matt's mom waved to us from the door as we climbed into the front cab. As soon as the doors shut, I turned to him, "So, Ma—"

Reading my mind, he cut me off in a flash. "Do not start calling me Mattie."

I grinned.

He flashed me an earnest pout. "Please? I don't like it."

Silence.

"At all." His jaw clenched as he stared out the windshield.

Taking pity on him, I smiled and patted his arm, "Okay. If you're sure."

He took a quick glance at me and put the truck into drive. "Yes. Very sure."

Once we hit the main road, he asked, "Did you have any nicknames as a kid?"

I groaned and buried my head in my hands. Heat started at the back of my neck and flooded up my cheeks.

Matt took a quick glance my way and laughed. "Oh, c'mon, how bad could it have been?"

I shook my head, dreading this moment. "Okay, here's the deal. Sean had trouble saying my name when we were little. It took my parents weeks to figure out when he was walking through the house yelling *Disney*, he was actually calling Lindsey."

He raised his eyebrows and waited.

"So, Disney evolved into the princesses—Cinderella, Sleeping Beauty, stuff like that."

His eyebrows crinkled, not understanding. "That's not too bad. What girl doesn't want to be a princess?"

Time to stop beating around the bush. "You're right, princess names were fine. But as I got older, they morphed into…dwarves. Then I had to draw the line."

The corner of his mouth quirked up. "Like Grumpy?"

I nodded. "Grumpy, Sleepy, Dopey. Then Sean started to make them up—Surly, Cranky, Bitchy—"

Matt had his lips pressed together, trying his best not to smile.

Once again, the stupid dwarf song popped into my head. *Hi ho, hi ho* my ass. I squeezed my fingers into my temples hoping to dislodge it. "My parents will occasionally bring it up, trying to be funny. But Sean still uses them just to piss me off."

"That's what brothers are for." His smirk told me he had taken equal delight in tormenting his sisters.

"Yeah, well, my parents didn't have to egg him on," I grumbled. Eager to get off the topic, I changed the subject to something more relevant. "Speaking of parents, your mom seems nice."

"Yeah, she's great." He shot me a sideways glance. "As you can tell, my dad's another story."

"Not really the warm, fuzzy type, is he?"

Matt snorted. "Far from it."

"Doesn't that make it hard for you to live there?"

He shrugged, keeping his eyes on the road. "It's not so bad. He acts like he doesn't want me fussing over him—but I know he appreciates it."

Fussing wasn't the word I would have chosen. Granted, I hadn't seen Matt in action, but I'm guessing autocratic might be closer to the mark. Never a good idea when dealing with a parent. I selected my next words carefully. "I've found, sometimes, when certain men are 'fussed over,' they rebel and behave in ways contradictory to their best interests."

I wasn't surprised to see his jaw twitch as he formulated a denial. "No, I think he'd be contradictory whether I was around or not."

"You may be right," I responded with an encouraging tone, "but he may also have trouble accepting you as the rule setter in his own home." With raised eyebrows and a slight shoulder shrug, I hoped to plant the seed without appearing too judgmental.

No response. Instead, he pointed to a spot along the side of the road. "Look. Mile marker seventy."

Okay. If he wanted to change the subject, I was game. Lightheartedly, I responded, "Hey, that's where we had our first date."

He chuckled, as I'd hoped, before growling, "Behave or I'll drop you off and this will be our last."

"Ha. Not likely. After seeing all those pixies today, I think I'm safe. No wonder you fell for me so fast."

He groaned and shot me a pained look. "I'm just glad my mom didn't have an affinity for bloodhounds. I shudder to think who I would have brought home then."

I patted his cheek with a giggle. *God, this weekend was going to be fun.* We spent the next hour talking about everything and anything, enjoying each other's company in the warm cocoon of his truck.

As we crossed into Vermont, my senses shot into overload. It was unbelievably beautiful! Snow coated the trees, pulling their branches over the road in a magical archway. Silver-white mountains surrounded us, rising up to a pure blue sky. Quaint little shops dotted the countryside. Instead of billboards, many of them had oversized sculptures promoting their wares—a giant bed outside a furniture store, an enormous bear advertised wooden lawn decorations. My face plastered against the window, I felt like a little kid.

"Having a good time?" Matt laughed at my obvious delight.

"It's so beautiful. Like a movie."

"I'm glad you approve. I hope the house lives up to your expectations."

"It'll be perfect because I'm with you." I grabbed his hand and gave it a squeeze. He squeezed back and winked, his dimple on full display.

The sun had started to dip below the mountain when we turned off the main road and up a private drive lined with three-foot snowdrifts. Passing a few scattered cabins, we slowed down as we approached a barely-plowed driveway.

"We're here," Matt announced. Bumping over the uneven ground, we made our way through the trees. In the clearing sat a delightful little house, faded grey with a bright blue door, surrounded by thick, dark woods.

"Ooow, I love it!" I opened the door of the cab and was hit with a frigid blast of air. "Gaah!" I slammed the door shut and reached for my coat.

Matt laughed as he climbed out. Grabbing our bags from the back, he slung them over his shoulder and dug a key out of his pocket. "C'mon, sissy. I'll race you to the door."

Jamming my arms into my sleeves, I wrapped the coat around me and sprinted through the snow and up the steps. Matt unlocked the door and flicked on the lights.

As we wiped our boots on the mat, I took a quick peek around.

The living room was charming, painted a warm caramel, comfortably furnished with overstuffed sofas the color of daylilies, a large brick fireplace and a big flat-screen TV. Through the back was a surprisingly elegant kitchen, with stainless steel appliances and granite countertops.

"When you said ski cabin, I expected more of a rustic shack. This is lovely. Your brother must do pretty well for himself."

"Well, it was more of a shack when Kevin bought it. We've made some improvements over the years. We Quincy boys are pretty handy."

"So I see."

Waving his hand, he said, "Quick tour…kitchen's back there. The dining room's off it to the left." Adjusting the bags on his shoulders, he nodded his head to the right and started walking. "Bedrooms are down here. There's a main bathroom—" he nodded to the first door in the hallway, "—a master bed and bath to the right, two rooms on the left, and this one's mine." He stopped at the end of the hallway and nudged the door open with his toe.

The room was deep green, with cream trim, a handsome maple dresser and a king-size mattress. It suited him perfectly.

"I hope you like it. It's plain but has the biggest bed."

"This is perfect." I couldn't wait to curl up with him for the next four days. No studying, no work, just me and Matt and a really big bed.

Chapter 22

We got up early the next morning, rented skis, and hit the slopes. Well, Matt skied, and I hit the slopes. Literally. It took him about two hours of patient instructions before I could navigate without falling.

By noon I'd learned how to "pizza and French fry" on the bunny slope—slowing down and speeding up by turning my ski tips in and out. Then, despite my vociferous protests, he took me on the chair lift to the top of the mountain. Convinced I would kill myself, I was pleasantly surprised to survive a few real trails. But by two o'clock, I was frozen and exhausted.

When we reached the bottom of the mountain, I sagged with relief, propping myself up on my poles. "Matt, this has been fun, but I think I've had enough."

"Are you sure? You're really starting to get the hang of it." He stretched his goggles to the top of his helmet, his eyes shining a happy amber. His nose and cheeks were a rosy pink and he looked like a little kid. Adorable.

Taking a deep, tired breath, I exhaled and nodded. He flashed me a sympathetic smile. "Okay. We'll make an early day of it since you're just a beginner. But we can't leave until I introduce you to *après* skiing."

I groaned. "What's that?"

With a wide grin, he pointed toward the base lodge. There was an enormous plate glass window emblazoned with a moonshine-drinking bear hunkered down by a fire pit. The sign over the door read *Sitting Après-tee Bar and Grill.*

"Après. It means after. Beer drinking is a requirement after skiing."

"Now, you're talking!" Marshaling the last of my energy, I followed him inside. We shed our layers, stuffed them into a locker, and headed into the bar. After ordering a round of cold drinks and hot snacks, we collapsed into a booth overlooking the mountain.

Ahh, heaven.

By the time the food came, my limbs had thawed out and my fingers had stopped burning. More tired than hungry, I nibbled on chicken wings, while Matt attacked a double cheeseburger, fries and slaw. His movements were fluid, controlled and utterly sexy. Every so often, he would glance up and smile and my heart would go thumpity-thump. He was, by far, the hottest guy there, which was saying something. The place was packed with attractive, well-dressed and obviously wealthy professionals. Glittery jewelry and high-tech gadgets flashed everywhere. It was a little intimidating.

"Your brother must be pretty successful to afford a place up here."

"Yeah, I guess." Matt's attention remained focused on his burger. "He heads the marketing department for a software company in Boston."

"And you said he's married?"

He nodded and swiped his mouth with a napkin. "His wife is a nice lady named Keri and they have two kids."

"And he's how much older than you?"

His brow furrowed as he thought a moment. "Almost ten years. My parents really spread us out."

"How about the others?"

He scraped the last of the coleslaw on to his fork, swallowed, and washed it down with a sip of beer. "Jen's next. She's six years older than me. Lives in Connecticut with her husband and three kids. And finally, Katie.

She's two years older, also married with a son, Bradley, who turned one last month. They live in Manhattan."

"Do you get to see them much?"

His mouth twisted. "Not really. We drive up to Boston Christmas Eve, so we can watch all the kids open their presents in the morning. It's pretty much the only time I see Kevin and his family. Since Jen and Katie live closer, they come over for the occasional weekend, but it's not the same."

"Yeah. My family's only twenty minutes away, but because of my schedule, I don't see them much. Sometimes Sean'll drop in and we'll just hang out, watch a movie or whatever. That's always a nice treat."

He reached his hand across the table to rub my knuckles and sighed. "You're lucky. I miss seeing Katie. Since we were closest in age, we did the most together. She was always there to give me advice and stuff. But she's pretty busy with Bradley now."

"It's good she'd got her life figured out. I love Sean, but he's such a slacker. Right now he's coaching high school lacrosse and refs youth sports events. I keep hoping he'll find a real job or a girlfriend, but he's happy just hanging out and goofing around."

"It'll come. Guys seem to take longer to find their path than girls."

"Yeah, I guess. You seem to have known what you wanted."

He shrugged. "My mom said I was born an old soul. I always knew my mind."

"Hmm. The very efficient Officer Quincy."

He rapped his fingers on the table twice. "That's me— a man of action. Decide on a plan and full speed ahead."

I shook my head. "I'm just the opposite. I need to gather data, weigh my options, consider all the pros and cons. Once I've made a decision, I'm good, but while trying to decide I drive my family and friends absolutely bonkers going back and forth. 'What if this? What if that?'"

"Not me. I see what needs to be done, and boom, I do it."

"No regrets? No second thoughts?"

He shook his head sharply. "Nope."

He sat there, exuding confidence. A very sexy look on a man. Especially my man. Finishing my beer, I fluttered my eyelashes. "Ready to go home?"

"Oh yeah." Without missing a beat, he drained his glass, threw down two twenties, and steered me toward the door.

This Man of Action thing had definite appeal.

***

We pulled up to the house and I groaned trying to exit the truck. "Oh, God, I'm so sore."

Matt walked around to my side and put a comforting arm around me. "Don't worry, Pix. I've got the perfect cure."

He swept me into his arms and carried me into the house. After placing me gently on the sofa he said, "Sit there and relax. I'll be back in a minute."

"What are you up to?"

"Shh. Don't worry, you'll like it."

He flashed me a dazzling grin before disappearing out the back door. After about five minutes he came back, blowing on his hands. "Damn, it's cold out there." Then he darted into the bedroom. This time he was only gone a moment before strolling back with my fuzzy, blue bathrobe over his arm.

"Strip."

I stared at him. "What?"

"Trust me. Strip." He threw my bathrobe over the arm of the sofa and kicked off his shoes.

I held up my hand, trying to rein him in. "Wait, you're going to get naked right here in the living room?"

He had a wicked grin on his face, "Who's gonna see?" Then he pulled his thermal shirt over his head. The sight of his bare chest could pretty much drive me to do anything. As he shoved down his pants, I pulled off my sweater and ski pants. Once we were both undressed, he handed me my bathrobe and carried me outside, onto a snow-covered deck.

My muscles screamed in protest until I spotted the hot tub. "Oh my God!"

"The perfect end to a day of skiing," Matt announced, his dimple peeking through the day's scruff.

"You are not kidding."

Matt put me down on a patch of deck he'd shoveled clear. He stripped off my robe, and before I had time to grow cold, submerged me in hundred-degree water.

The sky was black, the air was crisp, stars twinkled overhead and I was with my man. Heaven on a stick.

The jets soothed my aches and the heat lulled me into semi-consciousness. I closed my eyes and melted like chocolate on a hot stove.

"Feeling better?" he asked after a few minutes, stirring me from my tub-coma.

"Oh yeah." I smiled, as my breath came out in a frosty puff. "I could fall asleep and stay here all night."

He raised his head from the rim of the tub. "Oh really?" He lifted his leg and placed his bare foot on my naked thigh.

"I was kind of hoping–" he trailed off. His foot moved back and forth, back and forth, skimming my thigh's sensitive skin with his toes, mesmerizing me. As his foot inched closer and closer, I held my breath. Waiting. Pulsing with anticipation. "Yes?" The word slid out half whimpering, half begging.

With a male smirk, he scooted forward on his seat, nudging my legs apart. "I was hoping…maybe—"

The arch of his foot edged closer still until it rested against my core. With the slightest pressure he'd turned me dizzy, the sensation potent and overwhelming. My eyes closed and my head sank back against the edge of the tub. "Mmm. Hoping for what?"

"That you'd get me a beer," he announced and removed his foot.

My eyes shot open. "Whaaa?"

Laughing, he stood up. I couldn't help but sigh in admiration as water sluiced down his body, long and lean.

"Just kidding, Pixie-girl. I'm planning to take you to bed and make love to you for the next hour or so." He picked me up like I was a bath toy and carried me out of the tub. "And you know there's no deterring me when I settle on a plan."

Chapter 23

"It's raining."

Matt dropped the window shade in disgust and flopped back into bed.

"Mmflp," was all I could manage in response. Because, seriously, it was like the crack of dawn.

He lay there for a moment. Shifted. Waited another seven seconds and shifted again. Twelve seconds later, he swung off the bed. "I'm going to check the forecast. Maybe the temperature will drop and we can still get in some skiing."

This chipper, morning, side of Matt was not appreciated.

"Urmfel gom," I told the pillow, curling tighter under the covers. Sore from yesterday's adventures, I would have been perfectly content to stay inside and cuddle all day.

He was only gone about thirty seconds before striding back into the bedroom, "Well, it seems the temperature won't go below freezing all day, so no snow." He paused, and I waited for him to come to the obvious conclusion—climb back into bed. The end.

That's when I learned Matt wasn't much of a lay-around-the-house kind of guy.

"We can't ski, but we could drive to Manchester and see the outlets."

I peeked through heavy eyelids to see if he was serious. Yup, judging by his eager expression, he was. Shopping wasn't really my thing. Frankly, I was surprised it would interest him. His wardrobe was limited to jeans, sweaters and work boots. Not that I was complaining, I just didn't see him eagerly trooping through Michael Kors or Yankee Candle searching for treasures.

Sensing my lack of enthusiasm, he shot out another suggestion, "Or we could tour the breweries. There's a bunch around here—Long Trail, Magic Hat, Harpoon."

Hmmm, I'd been to a few breweries when visiting Lake George. They were usually converted barns or oversized garages—ugly, drafty, and dull. Sure, there was beer, but we could drink at home just as easily. Where it was private. And romantic. And dry.

I didn't react, hoping he'd get the hint. But no, he was determined to show me a good time.

"I know. We could drive to Quechee and see the gorge. With this rain, it should be a spectacular display."

Obviously, I would have to agree with one of his suggestions. "Fine." I sighed, rolling up to a seated position. "Let's go to Quechee."

His face lit up with an eager grin. "Great. I'll make you some coffee while you get dressed. Be sure to put on your boots. It may be wet out there."

***

It was. Wet.

Very, *very* wet.

And cold. But I had to admit it was a pretty awe-inspiring sight, seeing the cliffs drop into the gorge of raging water and ice.

A few other hardy souls were wandering around, but overall, we had the place to ourselves. Giggling like little kids who'd ditched their chaperones, we took turns pretending to fall over the railing and sending pictures to our friends.

Tiring of that, we found a brochure and read each other trivia facts—Matt's arm wrapped around me under the umbrella, to stave off my shivering. Eventually, even that wasn't enough, so we stopped in a cozy little restaurant for lunch. Sitting at a quiet table overlooking the thunderous water, we thawed out over the most delicious bowl of cheddar soup ever created.

I found the meal quite inspirational, and during our drive home announced, "Let's stop at a grocery store. I want to cook you dinner tonight."

He squinted at me before returning his attention to the road. "Are you sure? We could go out."

"No, I'd like to give you a treat."

"All right…" He sounded way too skeptical. Obviously, he thought all I could handle was Hot Pockets and grilled cheese. True, that's all I'd ever made for him, but still…he should have a little faith in me. Eager to surprise him, when we arrived at the grocery store, I sent him off to the wine section while I pulled together provisions.

Arriving at home, I ordered him to stay in the living room, determined to demonstrate my cooking prowess. He spent the next hour watching football, while I whipped up my favorite meal—chicken piccata with linguini, salad with homemade dressing and croutons, and a tasty dessert. Every so often, he would call out, asking if I needed help. Assuring him everything was under control, he'd turn back to his game, yelling at the screen. It made me feel oddly domesticated. The shocking part was, I liked it. A lot.

I set the dining room table, plated the meal, and poured us each a generous glass of wine. With a satisfied smile, I called out, "Dinner's ready."

"Great, I'm starving. I could eat a…" and he stopped short when he entered the room. "Wow, this smells really good!"

I found his look of surprise to be a little insulting. "I *am* a nutrition major, you know."

"But when you'd said your dad did all the cooking and you took after your mom, I just assumed…"

"You thought my cooking would suck, is that it?

"Yeah. Sort of." He had the grace to look sheepish. "Forgive me?" His lips curled and that damned dimple appeared. Call me shallow as a sidewalk puddle, but I could forgive a world of sins for that dimple.

Fortunately, he spent the rest of the meal groaning in appreciation. Stabbing the last piece of chicken and popping it into his mouth, he smiled at me like a contented cat. "Everything was truly delicious. Thank you."

"We're not done yet." I jumped up and raced into the kitchen. "I've still got dessert coming." Grabbing the tray I'd prepared earlier, I carried in the dessert—light, fluffy, golden Belgian waffles.

I rested the tray on the table and placed a plate in front of him. Dipping a spoon into a bowl I'd left warming on the stove, I drizzled ribbons of delicious chocolate over his waffle. Slowly, sensuously.

He locked eyes with mine and flashed a knowing smile.

"Good?" I purred, before dipping my finger into the chocolate and raising it to his mouth. He sucked it between his lips and a thrill shot right to my core.

"Mmm, real good." He tried to pull me onto his lap, but I danced away.

"Not yet. First the *piece de resistance*!" I whipped a shaker of confectionary sugar from behind my back, and cried, "Pixie dust!" sprinkling white powder over the plate.

His eyes twinkled until I gave a quick shake over his head. "Hey!"

"Don't worry, I'll clean it up." I plunked down onto his lap, wrapped my arms around his neck. Licked the sugar off his cheek. "Mmm, you're tasty."

His adorable dimple popped out and I thanked the magical dust for giving me such a fine-looking man.

With a devilish glint in his eye, he leaned past me and ran his finger through the chocolate. Nudging open the neckline of my loose-knit sweater, he proceeded to trail a line of sweetness from my jaw to my barely existent cleavage.

"Uh oh. I've spilled a little on you," he said with a grin. "Let me help you clean that up." He ran his tongue down my neck, raining licks and nibbles, slowly, meticulously cleaning every drop.

"This *is* a good dessert," he murmured, dipping his head into my now plunging neckline. "I may make you cook for me every night."

"*Make* me?" I snorted, before sinking my hands into his hair and pulling him closer. Closer. Downward.

Taking the hint, he tugged my sweater down, exposing more bare skin, and nuzzled further. He was millimeters from where I wanted him. Where I needed him. And he rumbled, "Oh yes, I may insist on it." And his mouth closed over my nipple.

"Oh, God, yes," I cried out.

He chuckled, but being a very smart man, he didn't stop. He pulled me closer and nosed his way to the other side, licking, sucking, teasing.

Through a delightful haze, I realized I was sitting in the dining room, letting Matt feast on me. The blinds weren't even fully closed for Heaven's sake. I had to admit it made the whole thing hotter.

So, I wiggled my ass to make sure he didn't lose focus. Judging by his groan, that wasn't an issue. But a girl couldn't be too careful.

While his tongue was working its magic, he slid a hand between my thighs and tickled his way along the seam of my jeans. *Ohh*, that felt good. "Should we take this into the bedroom?"

He shook his head, flicking across my sensitive peak. "I'm good here, thanks." He increased the pressure of his fingers over my mound, "Are you good?"

I felt like I was going to combust, so yeah, I was really good.

Without a word, he tipped us both backward in the chair and, with a quick swipe, turned off the light. "Much better. Now I don't have to share you with the neighbors."

Before I had a chance to respond, he yanked the sweater over my head and tossed it on the floor. Lifting me up, he scooted my butt onto the table, while I giggled like a loon.

"You'd better move those plates or you'll get sugar in your hair," he ordered.

Before I could react, he shoved the plates to the edge of the table with a clatter. Pressing me down, he levered his body over mine. Resting his weight on one hand, the other hovered over the bowl of warm chocolate. Without taking his eyes from mine, be scooped up a dollop of gooey goodness and dribbled it on each nipple.

"Look, little chocolate Kisses. My favorite." The heat in his expression could have melted granite. I shivered as he lowered his head—slowly, deliberately—watching his eyes darken, his mouth curl, and his tongue dip closer and closer to my skin.

When he finally made contact, we both moaned.

With a very thorough and deliberate tongue, he proceeded to lick every speck of chocolate off my skin.

Lord, help me, I was like a firecracker with a half-inch fuse. Matt barely had to touch me and I was ready to blow apart. Right there on the dining room table. Whatever became of prudish little Lindsay Andrews?

I guess she had never met Matt Quinsy.

Deciding it was high time I shared these dizzying sensations with my man, I reached down to unzip his jeans. But he grabbed my hands and stretched them above my head. "Oh, no. After cooking such a delicious meal, you get to relax." He kept my arms pinned overhead as he nibbled his way down. With his impossibly long arms, he was able to hold my wrists with his left hand and envelope my eager flesh with his hot mouth while I squirmed.

Desperate for contact, I twisted my head and kissed his cotton-covered bicep. It was all I could reach, but it wasn't enough. Frustrated, I gave it a nip.

"Right. This shirt needs to go," he grunted. Without releasing me, he yanked the offending garment over his head with his right hand and down to his left wrist. Switching hands, he shook the shirt off his arm and threw it on the floor. Then he dropped down to cover me on the table. Rubbing skin against skin, he gave me a deep, probing kiss.

"I can't get enough of you," he growled, grinding his jeans against mine. Heart pounding, lust building, I'd lost all ability to move. He slid his hands down my arms and reached for the button on my jeans. Knowing it would please him, I kept my arms overhead as he glided my pants and panties off my legs. I was a little embarrassed, stretched out on the table like Thanksgiving dinner, but the look in his eye had me trembling.

"Now this is a dessert." He pulled up his chair, grabbed me by the hips, and buried his face into my thighs.

Oh, GOD. I grabbed the top edge of the table and arched up to increase the pressure of his mouth. Not willing to let me control the pace, he stretched his arms over my torso and pressed me down with his elbows.

Then he increased the torment by flicking his thumbs over my nipples. In a ridiculously short time, he had me begging to climax.

"Not yet. Don't move," he ordered and strode out of the room. It reminded me of when he'd pulled me over and told me not to drive away. I certainly wasn't going to go anywhere now. My limbs were like overcooked spaghetti. Within four quick heartbeats, Matt strode back into the room, naked, foil packet in hand.

He planted a passionate kiss on me, before pulling back. He was quickly covered and buried deep inside me. "Are you okay?" he asked, suddenly realizing I was stretched out on a hard, wooden surface. "Do you want to move to the bedroom?"

In my blissful state, laying on a table didn't seem so bad. I raised my arms and drew him in. "I'm fine. Go for it."

Impatient and needy, he pulled me upright and hugged me close.

I wrapped my arms and legs around him and held on tightly. "I love that you're so big and strong."

"I love that you're such a bitty thing. You're like a little doll I can carry around, wherever I go."

He slid his hands under my butt and lifted me up. I braced my hands on his shoulders and tried to increase the friction. Through gritted teeth, I hissed, "You know where I want to go now, don't you?"

"Oh yeah, I do." Settling me back down on the table, he reached his hand between us as he pumped into me. It didn't take long until we were both skyrocketing into space.

Once we collapsed onto the table, breathing became an issue. Trapped between the hard surface under my spine and Matt's hard surface crushing my chest, I wheezed.

"Sorry Pix. Let me help you." The table creaked as he rolled to the side. Standing, he scooped me up and carried me into bed.

"S'okay" I mumbled, air-kissing him before drifting off into a deep, contented sleep.

Chapter 24

After another day of skiing, we were curled up on the couch drinking hot chocolate, watching a hokey eighties movie.

I was amazed how much fun I'd had on the slopes. After mastering the green trails, Matt convinced me to try Tuckered Out, his favorite blue trail.

Since it wasn't crowded – meaning I wouldn't crash into too many people—I agreed. As we traversed down, we'd stop at the scenic overlooks, make out, take pictures, ski some more, stop, laugh about my falls (there were only three, but one was spectacular – a complete 'yard sale,' he called it) kiss, and repeat.

I was in love. L.O.V.E. Love. I couldn't tell him because, jeez, we'd only been together for three months. But what more could I want? Matt was handsome, smart, funny. He had a job. He loved his family. The sex was incredible!

I was pretty certain he felt the same way, yet he hadn't said anything either. But he was a man of action, right? Maybe I could hint around and prod him into saying it first.

I padded into the kitchen to refill our mugs and settled back on the sofa. I stretched my legs over his lap and snuggled under his arm, inhaling the clean, spicy scent of his shaving cream. "This is such a wonderful little place. I love being here with you."

He kissed my head and ran his hand up and down my arm. "I love being here with you, too."

His voice rumbled in his chest when he talked. It reminded me of those hot summer nights when I'd listen to the thunder of an approaching storm. Powerful, yet soothing. Just another thing I loved about him. "This was a great idea, getting away from all our responsibilities. I feel like we're hiding from the world."

"Mmm. Me too. It's been perfect." He kissed me, his eyes as warm and brown as the hot chocolate.

"So, am I the first girl you've brought up to this little love nest of ours?" I grinned, confident in his response. Until he went still, his hand stopping in mid-stroke.

My heart gave a little pinch. Damn. Not the first.

"Uhhh, actually..." he stammered, taking my hand in his. I knew it would be bad because his gaze slid away from my face down to our hands. "I was here with Rachel."

Ugh. His stupid almost-fiancée. That hurt.

He shot me a worried glance. "It was the summer before our senior year. My brother had just bought this place. He wanted to put in the hot tub and asked me to help him build the deck. Rachel and I came up for a few days."

He pulled me close and tucked my head under his chin. His voice rumbled against my cheek as he continued. "My brother was here the whole time. And we were working on the deck pretty much dawn to dusk. So, it wasn't really romantic or anything." He paused to gauge my reaction. When I didn't respond he added, "Not like with you."

"Hmph." I was certainly glad to hear him say it, but he'd still dinged my fantasy.

"Anyway, that's how Rachel knew I could do renovations. I'd done a lot of work with my father over the years and she saw how easily it came to me. I enjoy working with my hands—don't get me wrong—I just didn't want to make it my life's work. I wanted to be a police officer." His voice grew low. "Since my plans didn't fit into hers…well, then we were done."

I could hear the echo of pain in his words. Now my stomach and my thoughts were twisted. Jealousy leapt to the front because stupid Rachel had been here with him first. Mad at her for breaking his heart. But relieved since her incredible selfishness left Matt free for me.

Sensing my turmoil, Matt gave me a hug.

"It's been much nicer here with you. You haven't begged me to buy you things or complained once that you're bored. You cooked me an amazing dinner." He kissed my head and pulled me even closer to him. "Yeah, I could definitely get used to this."

Feeling the warmth of his embrace, I realized I couldn't be mad at him. Disappointed, but not mad.

He threaded his fingers through mine and squeezed. "I only want to be here with you. Hell, I don't want to be anywhere without you."

He may not have come outright and said I love you, but it was pretty damn close. I could live with that for now. I kissed him gently on the lips and then tucked back into his chest, content to hear his heartbeat solid and steady in my ear.

With a satisfied growl, he ran his hand up and down my arm. Once. Twice. Then his fingers skimmed my breast – slowly, tentatively. When I didn't protest, he grew bolder.

He spent the rest of our final night together proving I was the one he wanted to be with.

Chapter 25

"I hate having to go back to civilization. Can't we just rob a bank and hide out here for a few years?"

"I have a feeling that might put a crimp in my law enforcement career."

"Yeah, I suppose," I sighed. It was our last day in Vermont and we had lazed around in bed for as long as possible. But knowing I would have a long drive back to Delaware, we grabbed a late breakfast at the local diner and hit the road. Sadness seeped into my heart as we left our cute little cabin behind. By the time we'd weaved our way to New York, I was depressed.

"When will I see you next? Is there any chance we could spend New Year's Eve together?"

He shot me a look like I was simple. Hmm, I hadn't seen that look in a while.

"Do you have any idea how much craziness happens on New Year's, Pix? The roads are a regular demolition derby. It's all hands on deck that night."

I sighed. "Sorry, I didn't think. Maybe I could come up the next day. We could start the year off with a bang," I said, half-joking, half hopeful.

His mouth quirked upward, but he shook his head. "Sorry, but my parents are pretty conservative. If you came up, you'd have to stay in Katie's room. I sure as hell can't have sex in my sister's bed." He shuddered.

"I guess we're too old to sneak off in my car," I trailed off, hoping he'd disagree.

"God, yeah. Once you top six-foot, hooking up in the back seat is not really a practical option."

Bummer. I stared out the window, watching icicles drip sad little tears off snow-covered roofs. And sighed again.

"How about this?" Matt tapped my leg, bringing my attention back. "My parents are heading down to Florida in mid-January. They visit friends there every year. You could stay with me for a few days. I'll show you around town, you could meet some of my friends..."

It sounded wonderful. But completely out of the question. "I'd love to, Matt, but it's Winter Session."

"Which means you should have plenty of free time. You take one class and have the rest of the day free, right? You could skip on a Friday and make it a long weekend."

I shook my head. "Not really. I'm taking two classes and working at the clinic. I can't go away and still get everything done."

"I work and still manage to come visit."

Ouch. His derisive tone stung a little, but I chose to overlook it. "I know. But in addition to seeing my clients, I'm putting in extra hours helping to get the new office set up. I want to make sure everything's perfect when it opens."

"Why is everything your responsibility? Isn't there a team of people working on it?"

"Sure, but they've entrusted the pediatric section to me. I want to prove I can do a good job. It's important."

"And I'm not?" he huffed.

I rolled my eyes. "Don't be silly, Of course you are."

"Silly."

A quick glance at his face and I knew I'd used the wrong word. "I didn't mean it like that. You *know* what I mean."

"No, I don't. We just had an amazing time together. I really like being with you and I think you like being with me..." His eyes fixed on my face before turning back toward the road.

"Of course I do." How could he even ask? It just wasn't that simple. But apparently, he thought it was.

"Then surely you can take a few days off—call in sick or tell them you'll work from home or something."

"Matt! I have two classes *every day*, cramming an entire semester of work into five weeks. Plus, I have to study and fit in twenty hours a week at NutraHealth to pay my rent. I can't afford to miss any days."

"Why do you have to study so hard? Isn't your job guaranteed?"

"Well, yeah, I guess. But I like learning. And I still have to do well. I can't blow off my responsibilities."

"But…"

"No, I can't!" Closing my eyes, I scrambled to come up with a compromise. The sun shone through my eyelids, illuminating a hazy red glow. Oddly soothing, it helped to marshal my thoughts.

"Look, I'll have some time off in early February before spring semester starts. We can get together then."

"February." His tone was flat. How could he infuse so much anger into one word?

"I know it sounds like a long time away, but it's not forever. After these two classes in January, and a full course load in spring, I graduate in May."

"And then what?" Matt growled.

He actually growled at me. I jerked in response. What was he getting at? "I told you. I'll be put in charge of the pediatric unit."

"Yeah," he repeated, with notable sarcasm, "And *then* what?"

My heart stuttered. "What do you mean?"

He stared at me. "Then what? You'll be working in Middlebury which is even further away and I'm still in New York."

Oh, God. I hadn't thought that far ahead. I'd been so focused on graduation, I never considered what would happen afterward. With a gulp, I squeezed out, "Yeah, I guess."

This time, he refused to look at me. His profile was frozen, except for a single muscle jumping in his jaw. There was dead silence. Then he sucked in a deep breath, cracked his neck to the left…right…and said, "What if you moved up to New York?"

"You mean when I graduate?"

He shrugged casually, but his voice sounded tight. "Or maybe before."

That came out of nowhere. "Before? Like quit school and move in with you?"

He shot me a quick look and in a perfectly rational voice, said, "Look, my sisters both went to college. Katie even got her MBA and worked for a year in the City. But then they got married and had kids and they both quit. So, I guess I'm asking, do you really need to continue with your master's, now that we're together?"

He couldn't be serious. A firestorm flashed through me. "What? C'mon, Matt, it's not the 1950s! You expect me to move in with you and sit around all day, cooking your meals and doing your laundry?"

With an offhanded wave, he said, "No, that's not what I meant. You can get a job and all. I guess I'm only wondering if you really need to finish your master's right now."

My chest gave a weird little quiver. I should throw away nearly two years of education and he'd let me *get* a job. Like it was a privilege he could bestow. When did my perfect, reasonable boyfriend turn into a male chauvinist pig? Did he take a blow to the head I wasn't aware of? I had trouble mounting an argument through the strange buzzing in my head.

He didn't notice because he kept talking. "Look, you're smart. You've got good experience. I was just thinking you could start looking for a job closer to Albany. Then if something came up before graduation…" he trailed off, with a shrug.

It was then all the comments he'd made over the past few months solidified in my head. 'You could cook me dinner. You don't have to work so hard in school. Your mother should have been home more.' The realization chilled me to the core. "You want me to cancel all my plans and have my world revolve around you. Is that it?"

"No, of course not. I just think if this relationship is going to move forward we have to start planning our future."

My mouth dropped open. I must have resembled a giant tuna being hauled into a boat. "And you think we could jumpstart our future by me dropping out of school. In my last semester. You know that's insane."

"Insane?" He glared at me again, his eyebrows forming one angry slash. "First I'm silly, now I'm insane."

"That's not what I'm saying." What was going on, here? Why was he being so ridiculous? Trying to keep my voice level, I said, "Let's take a step back. I'm sure we can come up with a workable solution."

"Workable for whom?" he nearly snarled. "The way I see it, I'm the one who always has to compromise. I came to Delaware for homecoming. I came down for Halloween. And again after Thanksgiving. Then I arranged a romantic vacation for us. Yet you can't take a few days out of your busy schedule to see me for over a month! I've made you a priority in my life and it seems like I'm nothing but an afterthought."

Jesus! I couldn't even formulate a response before he went off again, this time banging on the steering wheel. "I'm such a fool. I thought we had something special. I know it was special to *me*. I guess that's why I'm the one always dancing around your schedule like a trained monkey."

His anger, reverberating throughout the truck, had me shaking. "That's not true! Of course you're special to me. I love being with you."

His eyes locked with mine and he raised an eyebrow. "Do you? Can you prove it? Will you come visit me in January?"

I was trapped. I raked a hand through my hair in frustration. I knew what he wanted me to say, but I couldn't. I just did not have the time. We sat there in painful silence, watching the other cars race by, until he blurted out, "I knew this was a bad idea. You know what? Forget it." His hand slashed through the air. "I'm done."

"*What?*" I squeaked. "You're done with what?"

He smacked his fist on the steering wheel. "This. Us. It won't work. Obviously, you want what you want, and I don't fall into your plans." The look he shot me damn near stopped my heart. His lips pressed together, his jaw clenched tight. It was a wonder his teeth didn't crack.

I panicked "Oh, come on, Matt!" Tears blinded me as I tried to figure out how to stop this. "You're not being fair. I only have six more months till graduation."

"Yeah, but you work in Delaware. You *love* Delaware," he sneered. "And I work in New York. And I have to stay for my parents. So, where does that leave us? Exactly nowhere."

Peering out the windshield, he said gruffly, almost to himself, "We might as well end this right now."

My heart stopped beating. Right there, sitting in the front seat, my heart froze for about forty-five seconds. I couldn't breathe, I couldn't think. I'd just spent the most romantic, amazing four days of my entire life with him and he wanted to end it.

"You can't be serious," I choked out, fighting back hysteria. "You want to break up? Here? Now?"

"I don't want to. But I can't do this again, Linds. I really…like you, and I want to spend time with you. But that can't happen, can it?" He waved his hand between us. "*We* can't happen."

My hand pressed to my throat, I gulped for air. A roundhouse kick to the sternum wouldn't hurt this bad.

Meanwhile, his voice turned hollow. "Here's the thing, I know how incredibly hard it can be to be apart. Things may be fine now, but it can't last. Eventually, we'll get resentful, grow apart, or find someone else. Someone who can be there full-time. And one of us will be devastated." His Adam's apple bobbed as he swallowed hard. His eyes, cloudy, impaled me. "I can't go through this again. I just can't."

Oh, great. This is all Rachel's fault. She screwed him over and now I'm the bitch.

I stopped to take a deep breath. Sure, I didn't know how it would work out in the end, but plenty of people had long-distance relationships. We simply needed more time. More time to talk. To think. To plan.

My fingers twisted nervously in my lap, turning white at the knuckles, but kind of purply-red at the tips. I pulled them apart and tried to rub the circulation back in. "How about this…" I started, uncertain what exactly I was going to propose.

It didn't matter. He cut me off, his voice sharp. Imposing. "No. I'm not going to waste time on a relationship that's not going anywhere."

Talk about a zinger to the heart. "How can you say that?" I cried. "Who's to say it's not going anywhere?" I reached out to put my hand on his arm and he snatched it away.

"Bottom line. You are going to finish your degree. And once you do, are you planning to take a job in Middlebury?"

"Uhh, yeah, I guess. But—"

He flicked his hand at me—the bastard—cutting me off again.

"Forget it. I know where I stand. I know where you stand. And they are two hundred miles apart. Literally." He glowered at me and his eyes were hard.

Cold. I felt like I was going to throw up. There was nothing I could say.

***

We spent the last hour with nothing but the radio to break the silence. The pain in my heart was excruciating. I refused to break down in front of him, so I just stared out the window, my fingernails biting into my palms, struggling to hold it together until I was alone.

When we pulled up to his house, he quietly got out of the car, unpacked my bags, and loaded them into my car.

I stood by the truck, watching him, waiting for him to change his mind. Crack a smile. Say he was just kidding. But no, his mouth remained pressed tight.

Once he was finished, he turned toward me, eyes focused on the horizon. "Well, goodbye then," he said. No kiss. No final hug. No tears of regret.

I stared at him, willing him to look at me. See the pain he was causing and Change. His. Mind.

He said one word. Just one.

"I…" But he didn't finish. He didn't move.

Knowing I was seconds away from a complete breakdown, I yanked open the door, threw myself in the seat, and without a single wave goodbye, flew out of the driveway like I was being chased by the demons of hell.

Chapter 26

The next few weeks were agony. I could hardly drag myself out of bed. I stopped eating. I stopped showering, except when I had to go to work. I couldn't stop crying. I was an absolute mess.

I told myself I was being ridiculous. I'd barely known him for three months. This shouldn't hurt so badly. Yet I missed him down to my bones.

After such an amazing trip, how could he end it so cavalierly? Didn't he miss me? Didn't he want to try to work things out?

Apparently not, because I didn't hear from him again. Not on Christmas day. Not December twenty-sixth, twenty-seventh, and certainly not December thirty-first, since that was New Year's Eve and he was working. Dealing with all the "crazy people" who were *enjoying* the start of the New Year.

Not me. I sat home, wearing Matt's stupid academy t-shirt, eating coffee mocha ice cream, and crying my eyes out.

Every time I picked up my phone, I'd pray there'd be a text waiting for me. Apologizing. Blaming it on a full moon or his parents or trouble at work. Something! But there wasn't. Not a single damn word from him.

On New Year's Day, Gabby stopped over. Thankfully, I'd been able to avoid her all week. She and her mom always spent the holidays with family in New York City where she's from. But now my reprieve was over.

Two steps into my apartment, she gasped. "God, Lindsay, you look horrible! What happened?" Without waiting for an answer, she wrapped her arms around me.

I wriggled away and threw myself on the sofa. "Matt and I broke up," I moaned.

She handed me a tissue from the box on the table and settled next to me. "You're kidding. How come? The last I'd heard, you were having a fabulous time together in Vermont."

I blew my nose and wiped my face, trying to come up with the words. How could I explain how stupid I felt, falling for a guy who turned out to be an insensitive pig man? "I...we..." I waved my hand at her, helplessly.

Unfazed, she took the snotty tissue from me and tossed it on the mountain of others on my coffee table. Wrapping her hands around mine, she issued a direct order. "Spill."

I made a funny hiccup giggle sound. *She'd used her teacher-voice on me.*

Gabby smiled but remained silent. Waiting me out.

"You're right. We did have an amazing time together." I sighed, lowering my eyes to my hands. "We got along great and Matt was so romantic and…" I took a deep breath. Exhaled. And raised my eyes to hers. "I fell in love with him, Gabs! It was so perfect and I was so happy!" Tears bubbled over and I pulled my hand away to smear them off my cheeks.

Her eyes widened with concern. "I don't understand. What happened?" Then her face hardened. "Did he hurt you?"

I jerked upright, waving my hands to erase even the slightest possibility. "Oh, no, nothing like that." Then I slumped back into the cushions. "We were driving home, trying to figure out when we could see each other again. We're both busy and live so far apart; it wasn't going well. Then he started on a tirade about what are we going to do after I graduate and maybe I should move up to New York now. Forget all of my plans…maybe even give up on finishing my degree, because I wouldn't be working that long, anyway."

"You're kidding!" Her eyebrows disappeared into her hairline.

"I know. It's crazy, right?" I wiped my cheek on the shoulder of my shirt. "But the worst part is, I knew this would happen. Remember, at the tailgate, I told you I couldn't handle school and a relationship, and Ashley was all 'you could if you wanted to.' And I *did* want to. But I can't handle it. Or he couldn't. And now I'm totally wrecked, I can barely think straight. Gabs, what am I going to do?"

Gabby grabbed me as I ranted, and rocked me back and forth, "Shh, it's okay. You'll be okay."

"No. I won't! I miss him, so much." I snuffled again. "Maybe he's right. If we want to be together, maybe I should give a little. I could move up there, I guess…get a job somewhere." With a heavy sigh, I added, quietly, "It's no big deal."

She grabbed my shoulders and speared me with a fierce expression. "Lindsay Andrews, don't you dare sell yourself short. You love your work. And you are really good at what you do. If Matt can't see that then he isn't as fabulous as you think."

"I don't know. Maybe my job isn't that important."

She shook me. "Stop it! You've worked too hard toward this. He needs to respect your commitment. Why do you have to be the one to give up everything for him?

"But he has responsibilities up there—his job, his family."

"And you don't?"

That stopped me. Yeah, I have a job. And a family. They were just as important to me. Why couldn't he be supportive? Proud of me, even? Give me a chance to figure things out? I deserved the chance to follow my dreams. Right? Damn straight, I did!

I looked up and saw Gabby holding back a smile.

"I know what you're thinking," she hooted, rocking back and forth with glee.

"Yeah, Miss Smartypants. What am I thinking?"

The gleam in her eye grew to a grin that lit up her entire face. "You're thinking we should go out and celebrate how amazing you are. Fuck, Matt. Let's get wasted!"

So, we did.

***

Spending the afternoon toasting my phenomenalism was all well and good, until the next day. I woke up in an empty apartment, in an empty bed, and felt like crap. So, I wallowed. I was a wallower. Wrapped in abject misery, I spent the day wavering back and forth, questioning myself.

Was I doing the right thing? I loved Matt and wanted to be with him. There was no reason I couldn't find a position in New York. Maybe not as good as the one I was promised, but I could work my way up or go back later and finish my degree. Was I just being selfish?

Or was he? Because it really felt like *he* was.

He should respect my drive, my intelligence and my career. Six months wasn't too long to wait. I would graduate in May and then we could figure something out. I wasn't telling him to give up his job, was I?

No.

Plus, I really enjoyed what I did. I was good at it. I could make a real difference in the lives of the children. My priorities should count for something. Right?

I'd build up a solid wall of indignation; then I'd see my pixie skirt hanging in my closet and fall apart again.

I loved him. Yes, he was a bit of a chauvinist, but nobody's perfect. God knows I'm not. And I'd never met anyone as caring, responsible, sweet—when he wasn't being a jackass. Why did it have to come down to this one, impossibly important issue? Why couldn't we come up with a compromise?

Finally, two weeks into the semester, I caved. I couldn't help it. I texted him.

I miss you.

Three words. Simple, straightforward, not too needy sounding. Right? Maybe he missed me too. What if he wanted to make the first move but was too embarrassed?

It was possible, right?

But the response was…

Nothing.

No text, no calls, no email, no surprise visit where he begged forgiveness and we spent the next forty-eight hours entwined together in my bed.

Nothing.

So, I broke out another box of tissues, slapped on a pint and a half of concealer, and once again dragged myself to class.

Chapter 27

"Hey Linds, I'm having a party Saturday night. You wanna come?"

Sean called me on Wednesday. He sounded abnormally cheerful, so I knew he must have talked to mom. I'd visited the night before, looking for a home-cooked meal and some TLC.

My parents couldn't have been more supportive, telling me my education is the most important thing and to follow my dreams and when the time is right, a man will come along who will respect me and my career, and this will all be a fleeting memory.

It helped—not at all.

What I really wanted was for them to call Matt, yell at him for breaking my heart and get him to promise to be the bestest, most supportive boyfriend on the planet.

No. That would be epically embarrassing.

I really just wanted to know I was worthy of their love—since I wasn't worthy of Matt's.

No doubt they tried to prove it by getting Sean to perk up my spirits. I just wasn't sure I could face it.

"Uhh, I have a lot of work to do for Monday. Can I get back to you?"

"Good try, but I happen to know the university is closed for Martin Luther King. So, you'll have two solid days to recover."

Damn. I hadn't even realized we had a long weekend. If I'd known, I could have gone up to New York and been with Matt. Maybe we could have avoided this whole stupid fight. Maybe…

Oh God, I'm pathetic. As though that would have solved everything. He would still want me to drop out of school and…what? Move in with him? He lived with his parents, the big jerk. Where exactly was I going to go? Ha! Looks like Mr. Man of Action needed some practice planning things out.

"Linds?"

Gaah! Sean was waiting for an answer. Getting no response, he continued, "You don't have to bring anything. Just come out and have some fun."

Fun. *Blah*.

"Linds," he said in a surprisingly tender tone, "Please."

How could I say no? He only wanted me to feel better.

"Okay. I'll come."

***

The party was a very, very bad idea. Sean had invited a few guys and a bunch of couples to his grungy townhouse, and they all sat around talking, laughing, having a good time. Since I was not—having fun, nor a couple—I sat in the corner and drank.

A lot.

And got quietly, efficiently, and totally hammered.

It was almost midnight when the pizzas arrived. Everyone moved en masse to the kitchen to grab a bite to eat. Unwilling to move, I remained in my overstuffed chair in the living room, idly listening to their inane chatter. One of the irritatingly happy couples mentioned they were heading to the Poconos the next day to do some skiing.

Skiing.

Was there a more depressing sport on the planet? I pictured Matt patiently talking me through it, helping me master the lift. Then carrying me into the hot tub for "the best part of skiing," he'd said. Before breaking my heart and crushing my soul. He was a soul crusher, the miserable, pig bastard, with those big strong arms and kissable lips and dreamy amber eyes and **GOD** I missed him.

So, I did what lovesick people everywhere do. I drunk texted him.

It is martin luther and I don't worka dn I could com see you tomorrow and drive home Monday.

I slumped down in my chair and waited. A whole forty-five seconds.

Then I started tapping away again.

I miss you amd want to see you and we can mak it better and I can drive there tonigth or tommorrow but I'm drunk so tonight wuld not be good but just call me or tezt or something so I kno if I should come. Its Lindsay. Andrews. Pixie. Your litle pixie. Lindsay quinsy remember

Then thankfully, I passed out.

Chapter 28

The next morning, I wanted to die. Quick and painless would be nice, but I would have settled for an hour or two of slow agony if I knew for certain I'd slide into oblivion afterward.

My head was pounding, my mouth was a sewer hole of chum and Sharknado was twirling around in my stomach.

What the hell did I do to myself last night? I remembered being at Sean's place. There was drinking. And late-night pizza. And talk about a ski trip, and...

Oh CRAP!

I grabbed my phone, praying it was a dream.

Nope. More like a big hoary nightmare. There it was—in the sent messages. The most pathetic, drunken text I had ever sent.

I laid back in bed and quickly revised my prayer. Please, Lord, take me now.

I opened my eyes and groaned. I was still in my bedroom. Hungover, lonely, embarrassed and miserable, clutching the phone.

Realizing if I didn't get up, I would completely self-destruct; I dragged myself out of bed. My feet had just hit the floor when my phone buzzed. I screamed and dropped it on the floor.

Jeez, get a grip, girl. Pressing a hand to my temple, I picked it up, peered at the screen with one eye, and once again prayed for death.

Pix, we need to talk. Please let me know when you're awake.

I stared at it for almost fifteen minutes, alternating between terror and euphoria.

God, how desperately I wanted to talk to him, to hear his voice. To find out it was all a mistake.

But what if it wasn't?

What if he wanted to yell at me for my MDPTE (most drunken, pathetic text ever!).

I'd probably woken him up out of a sound sleep with my desperate, rambling text. He'd thought he'd gotten rid of me and now he'd gotten two texts in four days (three actually, since I'd sent two last night) and he obviously wanted to put a stop to it. A far more likely scenario.

Groaning, I thrashed around on the bed some more. Why hadn't he just texted what he wanted? Why ask me to call him? Was that some weird power plaything they teach in the police academy? Hostage recovery, gun safety and dumping a stalking ex-girlfriend?

Maybe if I waited long enough, he'd text again. Give me a hint as to what he wanted. *Yup, that's what I'd do.*

Determined, I slammed the phone onto my nightstand.

Picked it up, to make sure I hadn't broken it.

Placed it down carefully.

Got to my feet.

Grabbed my head to stop the hellacious pounding. And slowly oozed into the bathroom to clean myself up.

I started to feel human again after my shower. Resolved to demonstrate free will, I got dressed, brushed my hair, and headed into the kitchen without *once* glancing at my phone.

After three bites of dry toast, I caved. I walked into the bedroom, picked up the phone, and sighed.

Nothing.

A giant tear welled up in my eye and dribbled down my cheek. *I'm not strong enough to handle this.* I didn't ask for it. I wasn't looking for it. I had just been driving up the Thruway and suddenly he was there. And he had to be all charming and amazing and make me fall in love with him and then he turned into a complete jerk and I can't handle it.

Tears started pouring out, splashing on the screen—and the thought flashed in my mind I might actually short the damn thing out.

But before I could put it down, it buzzed, and I screamed again.

Matt's face appeared on the screen. It was a picture I'd taken of him in Vermont. He looked so happy. And now he was calling to slice me out of his life forever.

Oh, God.

I wiped the tears with the back of my hand, blew my nose, and pressed Talk.

"Hello?" At the sound of his rich, familiar voice, I collapsed on the bed. It was so precious to me; I didn't know if I could speak. This might be it, the last time I ever heard him. My chest collapsed, and I couldn't suck in enough air to answer.

"Hello?" he repeated.

I managed to force in a breath and croak out, "Hi."

I heard him exhale in relief. "Hey. Lindsay? It's Matt."

I couldn't help but smile. As if I'd have gotten so worked up over anyone else. *We might as well get this over with.* "Hi."

It was all I could manage. I heard a chair scrape on the other end. I guess he was uncomfortable too, trying to get settled.

"Umm," he stalled. "I wanted to talk to you." He inhaled and exhaled sharply. "I uhhh, wanted to say I'm sorry."

My heart stuttered in surprise and I shot up on the bed. "What?"

"I…I'm sorry. Really sorry. I miss you and I was a complete ass and I'm sorry."

For a second, my room lit up with sunbeams and rainbows and bluebirds flitting around. And then they faded. Because really, what had changed? Anything?

He must have noticed my silence and he began to talk. "See, here's the thing. I got your text on Tuesday and it tore me up. I was practically catatonic. I had been holed up in my bedroom, hiding from the world when my sister Katie called. She could tell I was a mess, so she invited me for a visit."

He paused. Took a breath.

"I got back this morning." Followed by more silence.

And? I was practically clawing at the bedspread, waiting to hear the rest.

"See, I told her about our conversation and—" Determined to torment me, he paused again. I was going to have to kill him.

But then…it happened. My miracle.

"The truth is, she called me a horse's ass and raked me over the coals for about twenty minutes. Turns out getting her MBA was the best thing she'd ever done. She took off a year when Bradley was born, but she plans to go back to work next month. She said she loves her family, but she's really good at what she does, and she can't wait to mix it up again on Wall Street."

Another deep breath from my sweet, possibly no longer ex-boyfriend, before his final confession. "I'm supposed to tell you I have no right to squash your dreams for my selfish reasons. You should finish your degree. And work wherever you want to work. And did I mention I'm a horse's ass?"

I tried to keep the grin off my face, "Yes, I think you did. But I'm happy to hear it again."

"I didn't mean to imply I expected you to sit at home, waiting to service my every need." When I didn't respond immediately, he added, "Although it would be nice."

I heard the humor in his voice but refused to smile. It was too soon. Scratching a spot of ice cream off my sweatpants, I whispered, "Your text terrified me today. I was afraid you were going to tell me to leave you alone."

"Oh God, no," he croaked. "I almost called you last night when I got your text. But you sounded pretty wasted and I was afraid you might not remember in the morning. So, I waited as long as I could today. I wasn't sure how you'd be feeling."

"I'm in pretty bad shape," I admitted, softly, flopping back onto my pillow.

"I'm sorry."

"I couldn't face calling you."

"I know. I'm sorry."

"I feel better now, though," I said, with a foolish grin.

"I'm glad. I feel better too." I could hear the relief in his voice.

"Good."

There was a pause and he said, "I was hoping…if it's okay…I'd love to make it up to you. I could, maybe, drive down there today?"

"Yeah?" My heartrate kicked up a notch.

"Mmm-hmm. If I leave right now, I could try and make it up to you this afternoon. And *maybe* even a few times tomorrow." He was smiling that sweet, seductive smile of his. I could hear it in his voice.

And suddenly the rainbows were back. The sunbeams. The tweeting birds, and unicorns and cute little puppies and kittens with big eyes and bright red ribbons around their necks. Thank the stars above, my man was back.

"YES! Yes, yes! Turn on your siren, flash your lights and get down here in record time, okay?"

His whoop was filled with as much joy as my response. "Yes, ma'am. I'm halfway to my truck already."

"Don't you need to pack?" I giggled.

"If you let me use your toothbrush, I can leave now. I don't anticipate needing too many clothes, do you?"

Chapter 29

In the end, he did pack a few things. Even so, he flew through my door in three hours, thirty-two minutes, kicked it shut with his foot, dropped his bag, and swung me up into his arms.

He wrapped me in a hug so tight, I almost passed out. Fortunately, he followed quickly with some pretty intense mouth-to-mouth and I recovered immediately.

Sweet Lord in Heaven, he felt good, I couldn't hold back tears.

Five strides and we were in my bedroom. Buttons popped, fabric flew, and we were flesh to flesh, finally, passionately, lovingly stroking, kissing each other.

"I love you, Lindsay." He wrapped his arms around me. "I'm truly sorry. I don't know how we are going to make this work, but I don't care. I love you. I don't want to live without you."

My heart puffed up like a balloon, threatening to explode. "I love you too, Matt." I pulled back to drink in his handsome face. "I think I've loved you since you first pulled me over. I'm so glad you came back."

"Me too."

Hours later, laying in what was left of my bed, my stomach growled.

"Sorry. I haven't been eating much lately. Do you mind if I grab a bowl of cereal or something?"

Matt laughed and planted a noisy kiss on my navel. "I have an idea. Let's go out to dinner. Have we even been on a proper date?"

I thought for a minute and then shook my head, "No, not really. Where should we go?"

"You decide."

In the end, we went to the Iron Bistro. It was a quiet place with private booths and a delicious menu. We were so embarrassingly mushy, we sat on the same side of the table, goofy smiles on our faces, staring into each other's eyes.

Matt ordered a blood-red steak and I requested the blackened salmon. While waiting for the entrees, Matt ran a knuckle down my cheek. His eyes were shadowed, his face serious.

"Linds, I *really* am proud of you. I want you to know that. I didn't mean to disparage you or your education."

His expression was so remorseful I was tempted to interrupt. But I wanted to hear more. I still wasn't sure what had happened to cause him to freak out like he did, and I desperately needed to know. Our whole future depended on it.

When I didn't respond, he drew in a bracing breath. Dropped his eyes and laced his fingers through mine. Then slowly raised his lashes to gaze into my face.

"I realized I loved you, and it terrified me," he admitted with a grim grin. "I just wanted to claim you before you could get away. I'd thought Rachel had broken my heart, but I realized that pain would be nothing compared to losing you."

He squeezed my hand tighter, pulling it closer into his chest. "I knew if I didn't make you mine now, immediately, someone in Delaware would realize how wonderful you are. He would meet your family and know your friends and not have to work crazy hours and I'd lose you."

He lowered his eyes and pressed a kiss to my knuckles. "I know it made me sound like a total douche bag. I realize it now."

Aww. My heart stuttered. He wasn't a pig man. He was just scared. And he loved me and I love him. It should be all that mattered.

But it wasn't.

There was still one concern he hadn't addressed. I slipped my hand out of his grasp and crossed my arms. "You do understand I intend to work, probably even once I have kids. That's pretty normal."

His hand, now unmoored, hovered between us. Then, he moved it to the table to draw circles in the droplets of his water glass. Pressing his lips together into a thin line, he gave a shrug. "I know. I'm fine with that."

My skin prickled. Wrong thing to say. "You're *fine* with that?"

His eyes grew wide and he threw up his hands. "No. Wait. That didn't come out right." Dragging a hand through his hair, he shifted his gaze across the room. "See, I always assumed my life would be like my parent's. The man works, the wife stays home. But I was just thinking in the abstract. I didn't stop to consider you…your plans."

He brought his eyes back to my face. "It won't happen again. You are entitled to a career and can work as long as you want."

Noticing my skeptic expression, his mouth twitched. "I swear, I'm a hundred percent supportive." He crossed his fingers over his heart and raised them like a boy scout. "And I'll even do dishes and laundry. Every day."

When I smiled, he gathered my hand in his again. "I'm such an idiot. Rachel and I broke up because she expected me to give up my dreams and I turned around and did the same to you. I feel horrible."

The pain encircling my chest for the past month finally started to loosen. I opened my mouth, needing to respond, desperate to ask the unanswered question, but he cut me off.

"Don't worry, we'll work this out. We have time. Just don't leave me for some idiot in fashion merchandising, okay?"

I tapped my lips, pretending to think it over, watching his eyebrows inched upward.

"Okay, no fashion guys," I answered, grudgingly.

He growled and pulled me closer. "Don't leave me for anyone. Ever." His eyes grew soft and scared. "Promise?"

I could barely squeeze the word out, past the lump in my chest. "Promise." Then kissed him. Hard.

Desperate to reassure him, and myself, we would be okay.

He cupped my face in his hand and then slid it behind my head, trapping me, inhaling me. The kiss turned languid, tender. It wasn't until I shivered from the strength of our emotions, he drew back. No longer sad, his eyes were dark with desire. And love.

Rubbing his cheek on my shoulder, he said in a husky voice, "You'll be great at your job. You are so impressively smart; I'd be a fool to stop you."

I drew back, confused, still hazy from his kiss. "You think I'm impressive?"

"Are you kidding? Absolutely. I sat in class with you and was completely lost. I'd glance over at you, expecting to see you glazed over, but you were busily scribbling notes and nodding away, like it all made sense.

This time, I shot him the 'simple' look. "Of course it made sense. It's what I've been doing for the past three years."

He looked adorably ashamed, his stupid dimple peeping out at me. "Yeah, I get it now. When you said you were studying nutrition, I guess I just thought it would be reading food labels or giving advice like eat your vegetables."

I shoved my shoulder into his and he grimaced. "Sorry. Lame, I know."

Before I could deride him further, the server approached with our entrees. We dug into our meal, feeding each other bites. He rubbed his palm on my thigh. I rested my cheek on his shoulder. It felt right. Perfect. Except for a steady undercurrent of uncertainty. Because, really, what *were* we going to do?

I hated to bring it up and ruin the mood, but by the time dessert came, I couldn't avoid it any longer. I put down my fork and sighed.

"Matt, how are we going to make this work? I don't like being apart from you. I miss you too much."

He pulled me close. "I know. I don't like it either. I've been giving it some thought"—he nuzzled his nose into my ear—"Some serious thought…and I've got an idea."

"Yeah?" A little flicker of hope flared to light.

"Yeah. It's too early to talk about, but I think I have a plan."

I raised my head, "You're not going to get me kicked out of school, are you?"

"No!" He seemed alarmed until he saw the smile on my face. "No, I learned my lesson. Next semester, you are going to focus on your studies, work your ass off, and finish at the top of your class. And in

May, I promise to be in the front row at graduation, cheering you on, like you just won the Kentucky Derby."

The Derby? What a weirdo. I neighed, tossed my head, and nipped his shoulder. He laughed and ran two fingers down my nose, "That's my pretty little filly."

Growing serious again, he cupped my face in his hands and stared deep into my eyes. "We will make this work, Lindsay. I promise. Just give me a few weeks to figure something out."

My chest felt too small to hold all the love welling in my heart. His look, his touch, his words, warmed me to my toes. I nodded, closing my eyes, so he couldn't see the tears suddenly bubbling up.

He dropped a quick kiss on my lips and tugged my arm. "Good. Now, let's get out of here. I want to spend the next few hours apologizing some more, okay?"

There was no way I'd turn down that offer.

***

Matt stayed over until late Monday. We had an amazing weekend hiding in my apartment, listening to the winter wind howling outside while we snuggled under the covers. It was just the two of us—warm and secluded—and it was magical.

But then Tuesday came, and he was gone, and I had a pit in my stomach the size of a grapefruit. Because, really, what were we going to do?

I would lay in my bed, night after night, turning the problem over in my head, never coming up with a satisfying conclusion.

I would finish getting my degree…in Delaware.

Then I'll get my dream job…in Delaware.

Near my family, whom I love…in Delaware.

While Matt—the man of my dreams—lived in New York.

He worked in New York.

His family needed him in New York.

I couldn't shake the fear he would realize there was no way to resolve our dilemma and leave me again. I couldn't bear the thought.

I tried to talk to him about it during our daily phone calls, but all he would say was not to worry. That he had an idea. Not a plan, per se, but an idea. When I'd press him, his infuriating response was, "I'll tell you about it when you get up here."

Since Matt's parents weren't due back from Florida for another few weeks, I was going up to his house as soon as Winter Session ended. He was going to show me his town. He'd been talking it up lately. I felt like he was trying to sell me on it, in case I decided to move there. I figured I would keep an open mind.

Chapter 30

I handed in my final paper for the semester and started walking back from class when my phone buzzed. It was Matt, but I was all bundled up from the cold, so I couldn't press the Talk button. Ducking into the closest building, I yanked off my fuzzy mittens and hit redial.

"Hey, handsome. How's it going?"

There was a slight pause before he answered. "Uhh, things are going okay. Did you finish your classes?"

"Yup, all done."

"How'd you do?"

"Good, I think."

"Of course you did. You really know your stuff."

"Thanks." I smiled into my damp, knitted scarf. He'd been much more supportive of my work lately. It was gratifying to realize how much our breakup had shaken him.

I turned toward a secluded corner near the stairwell and idly ran my fingers along the banister. "As soon as I get off the phone, I'm heading back to my apartment and can be on the road within the hour. I should be pulling into your place by three o'clock."

"Well, about that…" he started.

"Yeah?"

"There's been a change of plans."

I sagged against the wall as a shiver ran up my spine. That didn't sound good. "A change?" I parroted. "How come?"

"Well…my parents came back. From Florida. So, it would probably be better if I came down to Delaware."

"Okaaay?" That didn't sound so bad. Why was he being all weird? "Matt, is everything all right?"

He exhaled. "Yeah, it's fine. I …have some news."

My stomach started flopping around, doing a dying fish routine. "Good news or bad news?" I squeezed out.

"Good. I think. Surprising, for sure, but it's good. I'll tell you about it when I get there."

I was clutching the phone so tightly, my hand started to cramp. "Are you sure you don't want to tell me now?"

"No. It's good." His voice was stronger now. "I promise. For both of us."

"You're sure?"

I could hear his tone get lighter. "Yeah. Don't worry. I'll be there by dinner."

I did my best not to growl at him. "All right. I'll be waiting."

"Love you, Pix."

"Love you too." *You big jerk.*

I spent the rest of the afternoon fretting, cleaning my apartment, and buying groceries. Thinking I'd be spending a few days away, I had no food in the house, and now he was expecting dinner.

I'd hoped to have a nice few days relaxing after finals and then he goes and gets me all agitated. What kind of news could he have? Why couldn't he just tell me over the phone? It was infuriating.

There was only one solution. Kill him. When he arrived, I'd find out what his news was, fuck him senseless, and then kill him. But in the meantime, I whipped up a hearty pot roast. Just in case he was still alive to eat.

When he arrived a remarkable three hours and thirteen minutes later (do cops have a secret I'm-in-a-hurry-to-see-my-girlfriend code which allows them to speed?) he found me on the sofa, anxiously flipping channels on the TV.

I tried to read his expression, but he kept his face completely blank. Except for his eyes, which flared when he saw me. I stood up and he scooped me in his arms. Planting a big, sloppy kiss on my cheek, he hugged me and spun me around.

"I missed you."

Feeling my heart start to lighten a little, I smiled. "I missed you too. Now, what is your news?"

Determined to torment me, he kissed me, driving his tongue into my mouth and kicking my pulse up by about fifty beats. Once he felt I'd been properly greeted he put me back down on the ground, took off his coat, and sniffed. "Mmm, what do I smell? Pot roast?" He took a step toward the kitchen.

"Oh, hell, no," I growled, shoving him onto the sofa. "Spill. Now!"

He threw up his hands in feigned surprise. "Oh. The news? All right." He patted the cushion and I collapsed next to him.

Keeping his face neutral, he said, "Well, my parents came back from Florida with some interesting information."

"Yeah?" Figuring if I seemed too eager, he'd drag it out even more, I picked up the remote and started flicking through the channels again.

"They umm, bought a condo. They're moving down there. To live."

I dropped the remote. Now he had my attention. "They're moving to Florida?"

"Yeah, someplace near Fort Lauderdale. They adore it down there and want to be with their friends. They said they've been on the waiting list for a while, but never felt like they could leave me. My mom was worried I'd be lonely." He ran a hand through his hair, causing sections to spike out from his head. He seemed so dazed; I slid my arm around his shoulders. He leaned into me. "When I met you, they decided it was time. They went down there this month and picked out a place. It's maintenance-free, so I don't have to worry about dad doing too much." He shrugged, radiating helplessness. "They expect to move in by summer."

I gasped. "This summer? Wow. That's a surprise. What will you do?"

He shook his head slowly. "That's the thing. I don't know."

"Can you still live in the house?

He rocked forward, got to his feet, and ran his hands through his hair again, his expression desolate.

"Well, actually, no. You see, they need to sell it to pay for the new place."

It took a moment before the irony of the situation hit me. As a wicked smile crept up my face, I drawled, "So, poor Mattie Quinsy, Man of Action, has no plan for the future. In a few months, you will be all alone in New York with no family, no girlfriend to take care of you, and no place to live. Quite interesting."

He narrowed his eyes to glare at me. Being humbled didn't sit well with him. But I was enjoying it. "It seems you may need to reevaluate your planning skills."

He snorted. "Perhaps." Then he looked at me with puppy dog eyes and crooned, "I love you."

"Easy to say now." I rolled my eyes.

He assumed a more serious expression. "I really do. And I've been doing a lot of thinking these past few weeks.

"I'm sure you have. What exactly have you come up with?" My chest tightened. Our entire future was riding on his answer. I prayed it was a good one.

He scrubbed his face with the palm of his hand. "When my sister called me a horse's ass last month, I realized I'd made a huge mistake." He turned away, took two paces toward the kitchen, then paced back toward me. "It forced me to rethink my priorities."

He cracked his neck, a clear sign he was rattled. "So, I called Murph at the Delaware State Police. To find out what their requirements were." He shrugged one shoulder, as though perplexed. "It turns out, since I have a degree and have gone through police training already, I could apply for an accelerated placement. Here. In Delaware."

Wait...*what*? Was he saying what I thought he was saying? My mouth dropped open.

Clearing his throat, he said in an uncharacteristically uncertain voice, "When I called you this morning, I was actually at Delaware police headquarters, filling out the paperwork. There's no guarantee I'll get in, but I've got a good shot at it. It will take maybe six to eight months until I know for sure, but...I think I can be a Delaware State trooper."

I stared in amazement. "Are you saying you'd move down here to be with me?"

"Yes. In a heartbeat."

I leapt to my feet and wrapped myself around him. Absorbing his scent, his feel. Him.

"So, you'd work here—"

He nodded.

"And live here—"

He smiled that sexy, seductive smile, flashing that irresistible dimple. "If you'll have me. I don't want to impose."

"Well, you are a horse's ass."

"I know."

"But you are my horse's ass and I love you."

"I love you, too, Pix."

Epilogue

Eight months later, Matt hung his handsome blue and gold uniform in the closet of our new townhouse—pressed and ready for his upcoming induction into the Delaware State Police—and followed me downstairs. We'd spent the day lugging all our belongings over and were exhausted. Slumping into the living room, we collapsed on the couch, surrounded by towers of boxes.

"I'm never moving again," I moaned. "Who would have thought I could accumulate so much stuff in a tiny, little apartment."

"We did have to carry up my things too, remember." He got up and stretched his long arms over his head; his fingertips touching the ceiling. "It will be nice to sleep in my king-size bed again."

"Poor baby. You haven't fit too well in my little pixie-sized bed, eh?"

"I managed to make do." He dropped a kiss on my forehead before disappearing into the kitchen. I heard him rustling through one of the boxes. Glassware clinked. The refrigerator opened and nicked shut. A cork popped.

I smiled up at him as he reappeared carrying two coffee mugs and a bottle of champagne.

"Sorry." He held up the mugs with an abashed shrug. "These were all I could find."

Giggling, I took them from him. "It's perfect. Less likely to spill."

He filled them with the champagne; bubbles fizzed onto my fingers. Before I could hand him one, he put the bottle down and disappeared again. Too tired to ask what he was up to, I leaned back and closed my eyes. I heard more rustling, but within seconds, he was back. He dropped onto the couch, took his mug, and clinked it with mine.

"To our new life together," he whispered, his gaze warm and soft.

"To our new home," I said, my happiness bubbling over like the champagne. We took a sip, our eyes locked on each other. The world seemed to freeze in that perfect moment.

Then, Matt took my mug and placed both of them on the floor. He straightened, inhaled sharply and reached down into a bag at his feet. Pulling out a silvery wand, he waved it at me. Sparkling ribbons sailed toward my nose, then swayed backward. Before I could say a word, he lowered the wand and dropped to one knee.

My heart stopped.

"Pix?" he said, his eyes dark and serious. "I love you. So much. As we start this new chapter in our lives, I just…" He paused. Took my hand and raised it to his lips. Locked his eyes on mine until I could feel him in my soul. Rainbows and sunbeams shimmered in every corner of the room.

"Lindsay, will you be my wife?"

He placed the wand in my hand, and I saw a ring tied to the ribbons. A beautiful, sparkly gold and diamond ring that took my breath away. It blurred as tears flooded my eyes. My heart was so full, it choked my throat. No words could get through.

Matt shifted and made a funny, throat-clearing yelp.

Gaah, I hadn't answered him.

"Yes!" I screamed, throwing my arms around him, knocking us both flat. "Of course I'll marry you. You are the most wonderful, amazing man I have ever known. I couldn't ask for a better husband."

He took my face in his hands—his beautiful, magical hands—and kissed me slow and deep. "I love you, too." And in a voice full of wonder, said, "I can't believe I caught a pixie of my very own."

About The Author

Alleigh Burrows was enjoying a lovely drive up the NY Thruway when she noticed the flashing red and blue lights of a police car zooming up behind her. This real-life experience inspired her to write *Catching a Pixie,* a meet cute between a graduate student and a NY State Trooper. *Catching a Pixie* is Burrows second novel. Her first book, *Dare to Love,* an historical regency romance, earned her PAN membership in the Romance Writers of America.

Alleigh lives in Delaware with her husband and their sweet lump of a cat. Be sure to visit her website at AlleighBurrows.com or on Twitter @AlleighBurrows to see what her next project will be.

CPSIA information can be obtained
at www.ICGtesting.com
Printed in the USA
LVHW110056100920
665488LV00005B/1437